"Are you sure I'm going to need to learn how to do this?"

Ross asked.

Kathleen turned her head from the baby to find his face was dangerously close to hers. And when her eyes collided with his, her heart reacted with a strange little thump that quickly turned into a wild gallop.

"We, uh, don't know how long the snow and ice will be on. For all we know we may have to be her parents for several days."

Several days? He didn't know if he could survive being around this woman for several days. She already had him thinking things he shouldn't be thinking.

"I don't know anything about being a daddy," he said.

Her full lips curved into a smile. "I don't know how to be a mother, either. I guess we can learn together."

Dear Reader,

It's a brand-new year, and we at Silhouette Romance have a brand-new lineup of dashing heroes, winsome heroines and happy endings galore! Winter is the perfect season to curl up and read—you provide the hot cocoa, and we'll provide the good books!

We're proud to launch our new FABULOUS FATHERS series this month with Diana Palmer's *Emmett*. Each month, we'll feature a different hero in a heartwarming story about fatherhood. *Emmett* is a special book from a favorite author in more ways than one—it's Diana Palmer's fiftieth Silhouette novel, and it's part of the LONG, TALL TEXANS series, too!

This month, Stella Bagwell's HEARTLAND HOLIDAYS trilogy is completed with *New Year's Baby*. It's a truly emotional tale that brings the Gallagher clan's story to a satisfying conclusion.

Rounding out the month, we have Geeta Kingsley's *The Old-Fashioned Way,* Carolyn Monroe's *A Lovin' Spoonful,* Jude Randal's *Northern Manhunt,* and an inspiring romance from first-time Silhouette author Jeanne Rose, entitled *Believing in Angels*.

In the months to come, watch for Silhouette Romance titles by many of your favorite authors, including Annette Broadrick, Elizabeth August and Marie Ferrarella.

Here's to a sparkling New Year!

Anne Canadeo
Senior Editor
Silhouette Romance

NEW YEAR'S BABY
Stella Bagwell

Silhouette
ROMANCE™

Published by Silhouette Books New York

America's Publisher of Contemporary Romance

To Mary-Theresa Hussey, Melissa Jeglinski
and Eliza Shallcross for all their hard work
on this project.
Also, a special thank-you goes to my editor,
Valerie Hayward, for her wonderful guidance and
support throughout this Heartland Holidays trilogy.

SILHOUETTE BOOKS
300 E. 42nd St., New York, N.Y. 10017

NEW YEAR'S BABY

ISBN: 0-373-08915-5

First Silhouette Books printing January 1993

Printed in the U.S.A.

Books by Stella Bagwell

Silhouette Romance

Golden Glory #469
Moonlight Bandit #485
A Mist on the Mountain #510
Madeleine's Song #543
The Outsider #560
The New Kid in Town #587
Cactus Rose #621
Hillbilly Heart #634
Teach Me #657
The White Night #674
No Horsing Around #699
That Southern Touch #723
Gentle as a Lamb #748
A Practical Man #789
Precious Pretender #812
Done to Perfection #836
Rodeo Rider #878
*Their First Thanksgiving #903
*The Best Christmas Ever #909
*New Year's Baby #915

*Heartland Holidays trilogy

STELLA BAGWELL

lives with her husband and teenage son in south-eastern Oklahoma, where she says the weather is extreme and the people friendly. When she isn't writing romances, she enjoys horse racing and touring the countryside on a motorcycle.

Stella is very proud to know that she can give joy to others through her books. And now, thanks to the Oklahoma Library for the Blind in Oklahoma City, she is able to reach an even bigger audience. The library has transcribed her novels onto cassette tapes so that blind people across the state can also enjoy them.

Dear Readers,

Eating black-eyed peas and hog jowl is a New Year's Day tradition in my area of the country, and a must to ensure the coming year ahead will hold good luck! So I hope this New Year's Day you and your loved ones will enjoy peas and corn bread with your favorite meat dish (they go with just about everything) and that your coming year will be blessed with health and happiness!

Hope you enjoy,

Stella Bagwell

BLACK-EYED PEAS

1 lb dry black-eyed peas
4 to 5 thick slices smoked hog jowl
1 tsp salt

Wash peas, then place in large saucepan, along with hog jowl, salt and enough cold water to cover peas (at least two to three inches above ingredients). Cover pan and bring to rapid boil. Reduce heat to a very slow simmer. Cook for 1½ to 2 hours, or until peas are tender. Add hot water during cooking if peas become dry.

Added note: If hog jowl is unavailable in your area, smoked bacon will work in its place.

CORN BREAD

1 cup flour
¼ cup sugar
4 tsp baking powder
¾ tsp salt

1 cup yellow cornmeal
2 eggs
1 cup milk
¼ cup shortening

Mix flour with sugar, baking powder, salt and cornmeal. Add eggs, milk and shortening. Beat with mixer until just smooth. Pour into greased 10″ iron skillet. Bake at 425°F for 20 to 25 minutes. A glass or aluminum baking dish can be substituted for the skillet; however, skillet makes a better crust.

Chapter One

Kathleen Gallagher Hayes knotted the white towel between her breasts, then tilted her head toward the faint pinging noise at the bedroom window. Was that sleet?

Scurrying across the room on bare feet, she pulled back the heavy drapes. The warm moist air that had escaped the bathroom during her shower had misted the window. She wiped a hand over the glass, then peered into the dark night.

The window faced north and was partially shrouded by a huge gum tree. At the moment the bare branches had little effect in stopping the small bits of ice from viciously pelting the windowpane. She groaned aloud at the sight.

Oh, how could this happen tonight of all nights? It was New Year's Eve! Her family and friends were gathering for her brother Nick's engagement party.

She'd even bought a special bottle of champagne to add to the celebration.

Snatching up a red robe lying across the foot of the bed, Kathleen quickly slipped her arms into the sleeves and tied the belt at the waist. She hadn't noticed any precipitation before she'd gotten into the shower. Maybe the highway would still be clear enough for her to make it down the mountain safely.

At the front of the house, Kathleen stepped gingerly onto the small concrete porch. The latticework covering the north end had blocked out some of the sleet, but the steps and the sidewalk along the side of the house were coated with a clear glaze of ice. Kathleen could see it growing thicker by the minute.

Shivering, she carefully stepped into the house just in time to hear the phone ringing. She clutched the heavy robe against her as she hurried to answer it.

"Hello."

"Kathleen. Thank God you answered. We were afraid you'd already started over here in your car."

She instantly recognized her brother's voice. "Nick, I just got out of the shower. It's sleeting like crazy here. The ground is already covered!"

"I figured as much. It's snizzling here."

"Snizzling? Is that some weather term the army uses?"

He laughed. "No. It's a cross between snowing and freezing rain. I thought everyone knew that."

"I guess I'm just not as with it as you, dear brother," she answered dryly, then plunked herself down on the arm of a sofa. "So what am I going to do? I think the highway is probably already glazed over. Nick, I can't miss your and Allison's engagement party. If it hadn't been for me you might not even be engaged!"

Nick laughed. "Give me some credit, sis. After all, I am the man Allison fell in love with."

Kathleen smiled. Her brother sounded on top of the world and she couldn't be happier for him. "Yes, but don't forget that I gave her a little push in your direction. Now I can't even be there to celebrate with you." She groaned, then cursed. "Damn! Damn! I should never have come home today. I should have just stayed on the farm and worn some old rag to the party. At least I would have been there and not stranded up here!"

In the voice he used to train army recruits Nick barked at her, "Kathleen, don't even think of trying to make it over here to the farm tonight! You'll break your neck, or something worse."

Kathleen grimaced as disappointment flooded through her. "I have new tires on the car. Maybe if I just crept along at a snail's pace, I could make it."

"No! I forbid it and so does Dad. There's not a highway more hazardous than 71 when it's slick. And my engagement party isn't worth you sliding off the mountainside."

Kathleen knew he was right, but that didn't make her feel better. "I know. But I don't want to miss out on the merrymaking. I'm so thrilled that you and Allison are getting married. And Sam and Olivia have just gotten home from their honeymoon. It's New Year's Eve! I bought champagne! There's too much to celebrate for me to be stuck up here!"

"I know, honey. We want you to be here with us, too. But not at the expense of your safety."

"That's easy for you to say. You're there. I'm the one stuck up here alone!"

Sounding just as upset as his sister, Nick said, "Well, Sam and I could try coming after you in his pickup. It's a four-wheel drive. We might make it up the mountain to you, but I wouldn't promise you we'd make it back down."

He didn't sound very keen on the idea. And Kathleen knew it would be foolish to encourage her brothers to come after her. "No, it would be just as crazy for you two to try it as it would be for me. Allison and Olivia would kill me if something happened to either one of you. Besides, if it keeps this up very long the authorities will close the highway, anyway."

"We're really sorry, sis. We're going to miss having you here. Maybe you can make it tomorrow for dinner," he added hopefully.

Kathleen could hear music in the background and her father playing some sort of tickling game with Benjamin. The boy's giggling and squealing was punctuated with her father's deep laughter. It was easy for Kathleen to picture her family and friends gathered together in the old farmhouse, roasting marshmallows in the fireplace, dancing in the parlor and toasting Nick's engagement and the New Year with all sorts of food and drink. Knowing she was going to miss it all sent her spirits plummeting.

"Yes. Well, kiss Allison for me. And tell Mother and Daddy I'll see them tomorrow. If the road's clear, that is. Otherwise, don't worry about me. I have plenty of groceries in the pantry," she told her brother.

"We'll call you later this evening to see how you're faring," he promised, then added with a laugh, "Remember, sis, *you* have the champagne. If nothing else, dress yourself up and enjoy it."

"Alone?"

Nick chuckled. "If you drink the whole bottle you won't know you're alone."

"You're horrible," she said with a laugh.

"Bye, sis. Talk to you in a little bit. And don't go outside for any reason. We don't want anything happening to you."

Kathleen promised she wouldn't leave the house, then slowly hung up the telephone. Well, what was she going to do now? she asked herself.

Impulsively, she reached for the remote control and switched on the television set. A local weatherman was on the screen, tracking the ice storm by radar. From his predictions, it was going to be a nasty one, and Kathleen knew she might not be stuck here for just tonight. It might be several days before she could drive off the mountain—a fate that wasn't all that unusual in the steep Boston Mountains.

With a defeated sigh, she rose from the couch and headed to her bedroom. Her hair was still wet from the shower she'd taken earlier. She decided she would dry it, put on a bit of makeup and the new outfit she'd bought to wear tonight. From the looks of things, she was going to have to spend the evening alone, so she might as well make the best of it.

Ross Douglas considered it a miracle when he got the pickup he was driving onto the shoulder of the highway without sliding into the ravine below. And since it was only about fifty yards away from the driveway leading to his house, he considered himself lucky, indeed. He could walk the rest of the way, and worry about getting his vehicle later.

After depositing the keys in his jeans pocket, he zipped the heavy coat he was wearing up to his neck and tugged the baseball cap lower on his forehead. It was going to be a long, frigid walk, and as he slid out of the truck into the icy sleet and wind, he wondered how he could have given up warm southern Texas for this.

The climb to his house was incredibly slick. Several times he lost his footing and was forced to cling to branches and dried weeds on the roadside to keep from sliding back down the steep, winding mountain. No cars passed him, either going up or coming down. Ross supposed nobody but him had been stupid enough to get caught in this weather. Coming from the warm climes of San Antonio, Ross had ignored the weather forecast this morning, thinking a little snow couldn't be that much of a problem. Next time he'd listen!

Once he made it to the more-level driveway, the going was much easier. Ross quickened his pace, eager to get inside the house to warmth and the supper he had yet to have. Since it had been early in the afternoon when he'd left for Fort Smith, he hadn't thought about turning on the porch light. Now he wished the meager gaslight fixture in the yard was nearer to the front entrance of the house. He couldn't see a damn thing and he knew the steps, and more than likely the porch, too, were coated with ice.

He was digging the keys from his pocket when he spotted something on the porch sitting next to the door. As he gingerly made his way across the concrete floor, he saw that it was a box of some sort.

He hadn't left a box on the porch. Had a neighbor been by? Left something for him? Hell, Ross, you don't even know your neighbors yet, he reminded himself.

Careful not to slip, he unlocked the door, flipped on the light, then carried the box into the house and set in on the kitchen counter. Obviously, someone had wanted to give him something, he thought, as he shrugged out of his coat and tossed it over a kitchen chair.

Rubbing his hands together in an effort to warm them, he turned a wary eye on the box. It was made of cardboard, and the top flaps were tucked and neatly closed. Ross was hesitant to pull them open. Maybe one of his new colleagues had left it as some sort of prank, and balloons or something crazy would burst out all over the room.

But that didn't make much sense. Who would be out in an ice storm, especially on a mountain road, just to pull a practical joke?

Deciding to put his curiosity to rest before he made himself supper, he tugged back the flaps and looked inside. Ross frowned quizzically at the navy blue woollen material bundled inside the box. It was heavy and looked like a coat of some sort. Who in the world would be giving him a coat? He'd moved to Arkansas only two weeks ago and into this house more recently than that. No one around here even knew him, except for those at the school in Fort Smith who'd hired him.

He reached to take the coat from the box, then suddenly stopped as the folds of fabric pulled away to reveal what was underneath.

Dear God, it was a baby! A newborn baby! The sight was so shocking, so unexpected, that for long seconds Ross could only stare down at the tiny human with its scrunched-up face and thatch of fine dark hair.

Was it alive? The question galvanized him into frantic action. Jerking the coat aside, he lifted the child from its makeshift cradle.

The baby was wrapped in a towel that was stained from birth waste. To Ross's utter relief, the child let out a lusty squawl and squirmed in his arms.

For God's sake, how long had it been on his porch in below-freezing temperatures? Thirty minutes? An hour? It couldn't have been very long, he decided, because the box was dry and free of snow.

With the baby in his arms, he ran out to the living room, where the phone sat on a low end table. "Oh, hell!" he cursed, then slammed the receiver back on its hook before he even got it to his ear. The phone was useless. The phone company hadn't yet been out to hook up his line. It would be next week, they had told him. Next week would hardly help him now!

All right, calm down, Ross, he told himself. Don't panic! Think! What are you going to do? This baby obviously needs medical attention, or at least someone who knows how to care for a baby. You don't!

Fear plunged through him as he glanced down at the baby's wrinkled face. He had to do something! The child could be suffering from hypothermia!

Warm it! Yes, wrap it up and get it warm!

Ross ran back through the house to the bedroom and snatched a flannel shirt and a thick sweatshirt from the dresser. When he pulled the soiled towel from the baby, he discovered it was a girl. In a hasty inspection, she looked to be perfectly formed and unblemished, as far as he could tell.

With the tiny girl bundled in the shirts and tucked in the crook of his arm, Ross frantically paced around the room. As his mind churned, trying to formulate some sort of plan, the baby let out a loud cry, making Ross instinctively cuddle the newborn closer to his chest in an effort to warm her with his own body heat.

Dear God, what kind of person could have left this child on his doorstep, where it could easily have died from exposure.

Never mind that, Ross, he quickly told himself. You have more pressing questions to deal with at the moment. Like how are you going to get this baby off the mountain to someone who can care for it properly?

Who was he kidding? Short of walking five or six miles in freezing rain, there was no way to get down the mountain. This wasn't a heavily populated area, but it wasn't isolated, either. Although state highway 71 was no more than a hundred yards from his house, it was so steep and winding that he doubted a standard car or truck could drive on it in this weather.

This newborn infant didn't need to be exposed to the cold again after what she'd already been put through. So what did that leave? Neighbors? Could he possibly make it up the mountain?

The question had Ross literally racing to the front of the house and the picture window in the living room. He knew there weren't any houses close to him on the way down the mountain, but maybe there was one on the way up.

Silently praying, he swiped a hand over the frosted glass and peered across the front lawn to the highway, then upward through the dense woods. Faint lights flickered through the bared limbs and tree trunks, making Ross sigh with relief. Lights had to mean someone was there. Someone who could help him.

He put the baby down long enough to throw on a coat, hood and gloves. Then he bundled the baby in a heavy quilt and left the house.

A mixture of snow and sleet was being driven by a vicious north wind. The ice stung Ross's face, almost blinding him while the slick glaze under his boots made it slow going as he headed in the direction of the truck.

The frantic desperation Ross felt made everything inside him want to run, but he forced himself to creep safely along the driveway. He knew if he fell and broke his leg, he and the baby might both wind up dying from exposure.

When he finally reached the truck, he discovered the door handle was frozen. Ross banged on it several times with his fist before the ice broke loose enough to allow the latch to open. He was shivering and out of breath by the time he got the baby and himself into the cold interior.

Just let the engine start, he prayed as he twisted the key. Let him make it up to that house and to help.

The truck fired to life. With a sigh of relief Ross turned the heater on full blast, then wrapped the seat belt around the bundled baby as best he could. If there was one thing Ross was certain of, it was that the next few moments were going to be a rough ride.

Ross somehow managed to get the truck off the shoulder and onto the highway, but as soon as he did, it began sliding sideways. The more he gunned the motor in an effort to straighten it out, the more the tires spun helplessly on the ice.

After several failed attempts to move up the hill, he eased his foot off the gas, which had an equally disastrous effect. The truck began sliding backward, and Ross instinctively jammed on the brakes. However, the snow and ice made them useless and the truck continued to slip faster and faster down the steep, curving road.

"Hold on, baby. Hold on," Ross whispered, feeling more helpless than he ever had in his life.

Seeing they were headed straight toward a deep ravine, Ross made a split-second decision to wrench the steering wheel and deliberately ram the truck into the ditch.

For long moments after the truck came to a jarring halt, Ross clung to the steering wheel and drew in long, shuddering breaths. He was shaking with fear, not just for himself, but also for the baby who lay strapped in the seat beside him. He could have killed them both!

There was nothing left for him to do now but walk, he realized once he'd gathered his wits. Somewhere in the back of his mind he remembered warnings about not leaving a vehicle in a blizzard, but Ross also knew he couldn't sit here in a freezing truck waiting for help that might never come. The baby couldn't survive in this. He wasn't even sure he could.

Bits of ice pelted Ross in the face and eyes as he struggled to carry the baby up the mountain toward the faint lights flickering through the heavy woods. He was sure his face was frozen, along with his hands and feet. He'd never been this cold in his life, and he was afraid to imagine what the cold was doing to the baby. She was securely bundled in the heavy quilt, but it was quickly becoming covered with snow. Soon the dampness would seep through to the inner folds and onto the baby.

He had to hurry! He couldn't let anything happen to the new little life he carried in his arms.

Kathleen attached the dangling rhinestones to her earlobes, then stood back in front of a floor-length cheval mirror. She was dressed in winter white wool slacks with a matching cashmere sweater. Rhinestones were splashed across the bodice and round the cuffs at her wrists, giving the outfit a party look. Her hair was finally dry and lying in loose curls around her face and shoulders. Beneath the coal dark tresses, the outlandish earrings swung and glittered against her neck.

Not bad for a night on the old homestead, she thought with an impish laugh. Then she turned away from the mirror to add the final touch—a pair of silver high heels.

There was no way she was going to feel sorry for herself tonight, she thought as she left the bedroom. It was New Year's Eve. Tomorrow would begin a fresh year. And more than anything Kathleen wanted this coming year to be different from the past one. She was determined to begin it with a sparkle and a smile. It was time that her life went on. Good or bad, Kathleen believed, she was finally ready to face the future again.

She was in the kitchen, arranging an array of snacks on a lacquered tray, when a knock came at the front door. She couldn't imagine anyone being out on a night such as this. But perhaps Nick had decided to try to make it up here after all. He'd been known to do crazier things, she thought, as she hurried to answer the door.

Safety made her flip the porch light on, then look through the peephole. It wasn't Nick standing outside in the freezing cold. It was a man holding a bundle of some sort in his arms.

She opened the door as far as the safety latch would allow. "Can I help you?"

Ross's face felt so stiff he wasn't quite sure he could make his lips move enough to talk. "I'm Ross Douglas," he said after a moment. "I live just down the mountain from you."

Kathleen continued to study his face, or what little she could see of it under the hood of his olive drab army coat. Was he the person who'd recently purchased the old Mabry place? She'd passed it a couple of days ago and vaguely noticed someone moving in.

"Are you having some sort of trouble? Did you wreck your vehicle on the ice?" she asked.

Ross was becoming impatient. Good Lord, couldn't she see he was freezing? The baby was freezing! Why was she being so damn cautious? This wasn't Houston, or even New York City!

"No, ma'am. I need help. A phone. I have a baby here that—"

"A baby!" Kathleen gasped. Before he could say more, she hurriedly pulled the chain latch from the door. "Please come in," she urged, pushing aside the metal storm door to allow him to enter the house.

Ross stepped past her and into the blessedly warm room. It had taken him at least thirty minutes to make it to this house. As he'd slowly worked his way up the side of the wooded mountain, he'd not seen a solitary vehicle, and before this woman had answered the door, he'd begun to feel as if he and the baby were the only two humans left on earth.

Kathleen slammed the door shut against the icy wind, then turned anxiously to the man, who'd walked to the middle of the room, still holding onto the bundle in his arms. "Is something wrong with the baby?" she asked quickly. "Should I call an ambulance?"

His teeth chattered fiercely as he said, "Hell, lady, an ambulance couldn't make it up here!" He glanced down at the baby as he hurriedly peeled the quilt from it. "Besides, I don't know if the baby is all right or— she needs care! I think she's just been born!"

Stunned, Kathleen looked at him stupidly. Was the man out of his mind? Or had hypothermia settled in to make his thinking incoherent? She rushed over to them. "What do you mean, you don't know? Isn't it yours?" Kathleen's attention was caught by the thick head of hair and little cries. Her heart turned over as she looked at the baby, swaddled in a sweatshirt much too big for it.

Ross glanced up at Kathleen, but he was so distraught that the only thing that registered in his mind was a young face and long dark hair. "No, she's not mine. She's been abandoned—I don't know who she belongs to. Just call someone, damn it!"

The panic in his voice sent Kathleen racing to the phone. It wasn't until she'd picked up the receiver that it dawned on her she didn't know exactly what she was doing. "What—who do I call? We don't have emergency service here!"

Ross tossed the snow-covered quilt to the floor, then looked desperately around the room for something to use as a blanket.

"Call, uh, call the hospital. Surely someone there can tell us what we need to be doing for her!"

He spotted an afghan on the seat of a stuffed armchair. Snatching it up, he wrapped it around the baby and carried her over to a fireplace, where a fire burned low on the grate.

Kathleen's hands shook as she punched out the number of the nearest hospital, then she grabbed the pad and pencil she always kept near the phone.

"I need help!" she blurted when a female voice answered, then stopped suddenly as a wave of fresh fear rushed over her. "Yes, I'm still here," she said, trying to collect herself. "I, uh, we've had an emergency childbirth here and, uh—no, no, there's no mother." Oh Lord, she sounded insane! "I mean—there is, but the baby has been out in the cold and—" She paused and took a deep breath. "Yes, calm down. Yes, you're right. If you could just give us instructions—what to do for her until we can bring her in to a medical facility. What? Yes, I'll wait."

Kathleen slapped a hand over the receiver and looked at the man and baby. "They're switching me over to pediatrics. They wanted to know about the mother. Where is she?"

"How the hell should I know! This baby was on my front porch when I got home, and that's all I can tell you!"

Chapter Two

Ross was pacing back and forth in front of the fireplace by the time Kathleen got off the telephone.

"What do we do? What did they say?" He fired the questions at her as the baby began to cry.

Kathleen ripped the sheet of paper from the pad and hurried over to the stranger and the baby. "I've got it all here." She waved the paper at him. "There just happened to be a pediatrician making his rounds, so I talked with him. He said to take things one step at a time and everything would be fine."

"Fine? What does he know? He doesn't know this baby has been out in a blizzard!"

One of Kathleen's dark brows shot up. She didn't care for this man's attitude. Not one whit. "Yes, he does know. I told him."

"Then why is she crying?"

The baby's cries had grown louder with every passing second, and were now rising up over the adult voices. "I don't know. I've never had a baby!"

"Oh, my God," he yelled in disgust, "I find a woman and she's not a mother!"

If it hadn't been for the baby, Kathleen would have put him out of her house right then and there. "I don't even let people I know yell at me, mister, much less people I don't." Her eyes cut an angry path over his face. "Not every adult is a parent. Are you?"

Ross shook his head, ashamed that he'd let his emotions take over. "No, I'm not. And I'm sorry for yelling. But I've—been going a little bit crazy ever since I found her on the porch," he said, looking down at the crying baby in his arms.

Kathleen quickly reached for her. "We're going to take care of her," she said, trying her best to sound reassuring.

Ross released his hold on the baby, albeit reluctantly. In the past hour she'd come to feel like a natural part of him. As though in some strange way she'd become his child, not just a baby he'd found in a cardboard box.

"Oh—oh my," Kathleen gasped as she carried the child over to the long plush sofa. "You weren't kidding, were you? This really is a newborn infant," she said to him.

He followed her to the sofa, his face consumed with worry. "I don't know for sure, but it looks like she was born only a few hours ago."

Kathleen had noticed earlier that he'd referred to the baby as a girl, but she didn't know whether he'd merely said it out of panic or confusion. "She? Then it is a girl?" Kathleen asked, darting a quick glance over at the dark stranger, who seemed to be suddenly filling up her living room.

He nodded, then pushed off the hood of his coat. Kathleen watched the garment fall away to reveal a head of thick, dark hair and a set of rough, craggy features.

"I'm Kathleen Gallagher Hayes," she told him. "What's your name again?"

Quickly he closed the small gap between them to extend his hand. "Ross Douglas."

She reached out and for a brief moment his fingers closed around hers. They felt like ice, instantly reminding her that this man had made a trek up the mountain in an ice storm. "You're freezing! How long did it take you to make it up here?"

He shrugged and unzipped his coat. "I'm not sure. It seemed like forever."

Kathleen jerked her head toward the fireplace. "If you want to build up the fire, it might help to warm both of you up." She looked back at the child and felt a stir of panic in spite of the pediatrician's warning for her to remain calm and collected while dealing with the baby. "First he said to make sure she was breathing without difficulty. Like a wheeze or cough."

"And how do we know?"

"He said if she was able to cry freely, she was more than likely breathing freely."

"Well, she certainly seems to be doing that. So what next?" he wanted to know.

"We need to check her temperature. The doctor said she should feel warm, but not hot, and her skin should be a pinkish red, not ashen or blue. How does it look to you?"

Ross came back from tossing a couple of logs onto the low bed of coals in the fireplace. "Well, she doesn't look blue, but her face is pretty red."

Kathleen figured that was caused from her crying, but since she hadn't been a parent either, she could hardly say for sure. She ran her hands lightly over the baby's arms and legs. "She feels warm. I'll go find a thermometer."

She hurried out of the room, leaving Ross to watch over the baby. He tried quieting her with soothing words, but she ignored the sound of his voice and kept on crying.

Frantic to hush her, Ross picked her up and cradled her in the crook of his arm. Thankfully, the contact with his body seemed to pacify her somewhat, and slowly her cries turned to faint whimpers.

Ross let out a heavy sigh and raked his hand through the damp hair falling over his forehead. He was a man who worked around children everyday, but they were the teenage kind. They weighed more than a few pounds, could digest anything that went under the heading of food and could communicate in their own strange ways. Teenagers were nothing like this tiny life he held in his arms. This child had thrown him for a loop!

Kathleen hurried back into the room with a thermometer in her hand. "I don't have the kind that you use on babies, but the doctor said we could use the armpit method in this circumstance."

Both Ross and Kathleen gave a sigh of relief when they'd taken the baby's temperature and it registered normal.

"Well, now that we know she's not suffering from hypothermia, she needs to be cleaned and fed,"

Kathleen said, glancing at the hasty notes she'd scratched during her conversation with the doctor.

"Do you know how to do that?" he asked.

Kathleen could hear the desperate edge in his voice. She was feeling that same desperation, but she knew it wouldn't do for either of them to give in to it. For now she and this man would have to do the best they could and hope it would be enough.

"I'm going to give it my best shot," she said with far more confidence than she felt.

Ross looked at her with renewed hope. "You've cared for children before? Baby-sat?"

A classroom of twenty-five students sometimes felt as if she were baby-sitting, she thought. "Yes, but not for an infant like this."

"Me, neither," he muttered. "They were all a lot—" he measured off a space with his hands "—a lot bigger than her."

Kathleen looked back at him and felt a faint flutter in the region of her heart. Ross Douglas was dark, brawny and utterly male. He was a man who looked like he knew much more about making a baby than taking care of one.

The thought tinged her cheeks with color as she replied, "Well, I think I have some books that might help us."

Books. Ross groaned, but not so that Kathleen Hayes could hear him. She was already on the way out of the room. After those books, he supposed. Hellfire, he muttered to himself, she was a grown, mature woman. She should know about babies. Women were supposed to have that internal thing that automatically clicked on when they had a child.

But Kathleen Hayes hadn't had a child, he reminded himself. So he could hardly blame her for not knowing. But damn it, he'd never felt quite this helpless in his whole life. He knew he was being irrational and tried to calm down. It made no sense to take his anger and frustration out on this woman. He looked at the baby, then shook his head. "Hold on, little girl, and I'll try my best not to let anything happen to you."

In the study, Kathleen frantically scanned a row of books. Once she found the titles she was looking for, she jerked them from the shelves and hurried back to the living room.

Ross Douglas was still by the fire and the baby was still in his arms. He'd said he'd never had a baby, she mused. But he didn't hold the child with the usual awkwardness men had when dealing with infants.

The observation took her thoughts a step further, to whether the man had a wife. He looked to be somewhere in his late twenties, certainly an age where most men had already settled into the role of husband. But he didn't appear to have that attached look about him that married men usually did.

At the moment, whether Ross Douglas was attached or unattached was hardly important, she told herself as she joined him on the hearth. They had a baby to attend to.

"This book about childbirth and baby care should tell us a few things," she said, hurriedly flipping the pages. She'd purchased the book when she and Greg had planned on starting a family. Unfortunately, she'd never been given the chance to use it. She'd never conceived, and then Greg had been killed. "It's obvious she needs to be washed, and something needs to be done with her umbilical cord, otherwise it will heal in an ugly shape.''

Ross grimaced. "Right now I'm not worried whether she'll be able to wear a bikini when she's a teenager. I want her to eat!''

Kathleen gave him a sidelong glance that told him she didn't appreciate his lack of patience. "So do I, Mr. Douglas. But we can't very well give her plain old cow's milk!''

"Why not?''

Kathleen groaned at his innocent question. "Because it's too hard to digest. Babies don't drink that sort of milk until—well, way down the road from now. The doctor gave me a make-do formula that I can mix up until this storm is over and we can get to town.''

The baby began to cry in earnest again, and Ross gently rocked her in an effort to quieten her. "Even if you know what to feed her, how are you going to give it to her? Do you have a baby bottle around here?''

Kathleen ignored his questions and kept reading. Ross wanted to curse a blue streak at her. He was a man of action and this waiting around while Kathleen Hayes educated herself about babies was driving him mad.

Finally she looked up at him and blinked, as though his question had just registered with her. "What? A bottle? Oh, yes, I believe I do. One of my friends with a baby left a bottle here some time ago.'' She motioned for him to follow her out of the room. "Come on. We'll take her to the kitchen and I'll start gathering things together.''

Ross followed her through the house, his eyes flickering from her to the large rooms they passed through. The house was opulent compared to the one he'd just moved into. It was furnished with modern, expensive furniture, deep, thick carpeting, draperies that show-cased rather than covered the windows. Oil paintings decorated the walls, while fragile art pieces and potted plants sat here and there in carefully chosen spots.

Still, the house couldn't hold a candle to Kathleen Gallagher Hayes, he realized. She was tall and long legged, her figure lushly curved in all the right places. Her nearly black hair hung to the middle of her back in a fall of silky curls, and as she walked ahead of him, the sweet scent of jasmine trailed after her.

Earlier, when he'd started up the mountain with the baby, he had prayed to find a woman in this house. Well, he'd found one all right, he thought. But was she the kind of woman he'd been praying for?

"Were you planning to go out tonight?" he asked. Surely she didn't sit around the house dressed as she was now.

"Yes. To my family's house. We're having an engagement party for my brother tonight. I was getting ready to go when the sleet started."

She glanced back over her shoulder at him and smiled, dazzling Ross with the sudden transformation of her features. "And what about you? Were you planning to party, too?" she asked him.

He shook his head. "No. I'm still in the process of moving. I was going to unpack boxes." He looked at the baby girl in his arms. It was still hard for him to believe that all this was happening. "I guess I ended up unpacking the most important one, though, didn't I?"

"Thank God you did," Kathleen exclaimed. "I can't bear to think the baby was out in the cold. Do you have any idea how long she might have been there?"

She hurried into the kitchen and flipped on the overhead lights. Ross followed her to a work counter. "Not really. I drove into Fort Smith sometime before noon and didn't get back until the storm hit. She could have been left there anytime during the afternoon."

Kathleen shuddered at the thought. "Well, it will be up to the authorities to figure out who might have done this. But let's take care of her first before we bother calling the sheriff, or whomever. Do you agree?"

Ross nodded. "Yes, I agree. Besides, the authorities can't get up here to her, and we certainly can't take her down. Not tonight, at least. And even if we could, I don't think it would be good for her to go back out into the cold. The weather out there isn't fit for human or beast, much less a newborn infant."

"You're right. We'll just do the best we can until we can get her into the city."

His eyes on the baby, he said, "I guess we'll have to be her mommy and daddy for right now."

Ross Douglas couldn't know how his words struck her. He couldn't know how often Kathleen had prayed to become a mother and how she had grieved with everything inside of her when she'd realized she couldn't bear children. Now, through some crazy twist of fate, she had a baby needing her care.

She gave him and the baby a quick glance as she tried to figure out the strange surge of emotions welling up inside her. "Well," she said, her voice unexpectedly husky, "if you're okay holding her, I'll get what we need to clean her."

Kathleen had turned and taken a step away from him when he practically shouted, "A bath? I thought we were going to feed her!"

Frustrated, she turned back to him. "We are, Mr. Douglas. If you'll just calm down and think about it, you'll see that she needs to be bathed before she eats."

Ross watched the rhinestones on her wrists sparkle as she jammed her fists on either side of her waist. This woman, he realized, looked the furthest thing from a mother that he could think of. She looked like a woman just ready and waiting to seduce the man she wanted.

"Oh, and how did you come to that deduction?" he asked. "Is that what the doctor said to do?"

She drew in a long, bracing breath. "He didn't say. He just instructed me on how to wash her and feed her. But I do have enough common sense to know that once she eats, she'll more than likely go to sleep. A bath would disturb her."

"Look, Ms. Hayes, like I told you a minute ago, I don't know how long she might have been on my porch. And I sure don't know how long it's been since she was born. It could have been hours and hours ago. The little thing could be starving to death!"

Kathleen's frustration with the man flew out the window as she watched his other arm come up to cradle the baby in a totally protective gesture. How could she not be touched by his obvious compassion?

She crossed the few steps between them and gently brushed her fingers across the baby's head. "Mr. Douglas," she began, trying her best to sound reassuring, "I am woman enough to know that a mother's milk isn't always present when a baby is born.

Sometimes it's several hours before the—uh, well, before the baby actually receives milk.''

Although her face was bent over the baby's, Ross could see a blush spreading across her cheek. Apparently she wasn't comfortable discussing such basic things as a woman's breasts with a man. But as far as that went, he wasn't, either. Not because it affronted him, but because it told him that even though he was twenty-nine years old, there were things about a woman's body that he didn't know. Especially when it came to childbirth. Well, Ross, you never professed to know everything, did you?

Kathleen kept waiting for him to say something. When he didn't, she lifted her eyes to his face and was instantly jolted with sensations. Gray was supposed to be a cool color, she thought, but Ross Douglas's eyes were anything but cool. She could almost feel their warmth sliding over her face, her hair, her throat and finally her lips.

"Mr. Douglas—" she began, only to stop when he shook his head.

"It's Ross, ma'am," he said. "I figure we might as well be on a first-name basis."

Suddenly she was quivering and she didn't know why. It wasn't because of his voice, or the hot look in his eyes. And it wasn't because he wanted her to call him Ross. It was something within her, something that she'd thought had died along with her husband. But this man's closeness, his scent, his rough maleness was sparking it back to life. And scaring Kathleen in the process.

"Okay, Ross," she said, taking a step away while trying to give him a casual smile. "So—so I'd better...get the things for the baby."

This time Kathleen didn't wait for him to agree. She quickly turned and left the room.

Her high heels made a tapping noise on the tile. Ross watched her leave, saw the rhythmic movement of her hips, the sway of her hair as she moved her head. She was an enticing sight, to say the least, he thought. He couldn't ever remember seeing a woman with such ivory white skin, dark green-brown eyes and hair the color of midnight. He'd stumbled onto an Irish rose in the middle of an ice storm. And he wasn't quite sure if he'd been cursed or blessed.

Chapter Three

Kathleen returned to the kitchen after a few minutes, carrying an armful of blankets and towels. After making a pad with them on the kitchen table, she hurriedly gathered warm water and mild soap.

While she scurried around the room, Ross paced from one end of it to the other. He'd never known having a baby could leave a man so helpless and overwhelmed. No matter that this baby had come to him under extreme circumstances, he felt just as responsible for her at this moment as he would if she'd truly been his.

"Okay, I think everything is ready. Put her on the blankets," Kathleen instructed him.

Ross placed the baby on the pad of blankets, only to have her immediately begin screaming with red-faced fury, her little arms waving rigidly at her sides.

"Is she warm enough? What's wrong with her?" he asked as he stared helplessly at the infant.

Kathleen scarcely registered his question as she pulled away the afghan and began to examine the baby. She believed Ross Douglas was right in saying she might be only hours old. The umbilical cord had been raggedly cut and left untied. Neither had the birthing fluids been thoroughly washed from her skin or hair. Kathleen wanted to burst into tears at the pathetic way in which this child had been welcomed to the world.

She didn't realize she'd made a sound, but she must have, because suddenly Ross Douglas was touching her shoulder.

"What's the matter? Are you crying, too?"

Swallowing the lump in her throat, she quickly shook her head. "I'm—I can't bear to see how this precious little thing has been treated. Tossed away like some old, unwanted rag." She reached up and wiped away the tears that had fallen onto her cheeks. "How could someone do this? Why did God allow it?"

Ross knew exactly what this woman was feeling. He'd felt the very same thing when he'd pulled the baby from the cardboard box. His hand tightened on her shoulder as he said, "Maybe God allowed it because he thought she deserved parents who would really love her."

Kathleen had to believe that, because she certainly didn't want to believe in suffering of any kind. "Yes, you must be right. And we have her now. That's all that matters."

With fresh determination, she went to work washing the baby. And as the signs of waste began to disappear, so did Kathleen's tears. This baby was loved, she told herself fiercely. Because she loved it.

"She's still crying," Ross said, as Kathleen continued to wash and rinse the baby's thatch of dark hair. "Do you think something is wrong with her?"

From the moment Kathleen had laid the baby on the padded table, Ross had taken up a position at her left shoulder. All the time she'd been washing the baby, Kathleen had tried not to notice his nearness, but it was terribly hard to do when he was standing so close she could feel the heat from his body.

"Going by what the doctor said, she seems all right. And she sounds like she has a healthy set of lungs, so that's good."

"But it couldn't be good for her to cry like this," Ross said anxiously.

"From what I can remember my mother telling me, it's pretty normal. She said my brother Nick screamed for the first three months of his life with the colic, and he turned out so healthy it's practically disgusting."

He watched as she finished washing the child from head to toe, then dried every wrinkle with exceptional care. She seemed to handle the child with confidence for someone who'd never had a baby before.

"I don't suppose you have any diapers around here," he mused aloud. "What are we going to use?"

Kathleen gave him a brief smile. "You're going to make some while I mix up the formula."

He stared at her in amazement. "Me? I can't make a diaper. I barely know how to put one on a baby, much less make one!"

If the baby's cries hadn't been so disturbing, she probably would have laughed at the panicked look on his face. How could men bravely face an enemy in battle, but want to turn tail and run when confronted with caring for a newborn?

"Surely it can't be that hard," she assured him. "When I went after the blankets, I found a white sheet. You can cut it into large squares while I fix her a bottle."

Ross would do anything to finally get a bottle in the baby's mouth. He somehow felt that once he saw her eating, he'd know that she was really okay.

"So, show me what to do," he said, resigning himself to the task.

Kathleen got the sheet and scissors and cut a pattern for him. While he made the diapers, she pinned a thick hand towel onto the baby for the time being, then wrapped her loosely in a flannel sheet.

"She looks beautiful," Kathleen said, her voice tender as she dabbed a little baby oil onto her fingertips and smoothed the dark baby hair.

"You know, the more I think about the whole thing, the more I wonder what kind of woman could give birth, then just leave the child with a stranger," Ross said with angry dismay.

Kathleen looked up at him, her expression suddenly thoughtful. "Maybe it wasn't a stranger. Maybe it was someone who knew you," she said.

He brushed her suggestion aside with a doubtful shake of his head. "I only moved here two weeks ago. The only people I know are the ones I'll be working with."

"Where is that?"

"Fort Smith. I'm a high school baseball coach and history teacher."

So Ross Douglas was a teacher, she thought curiously. He certainly fit the coach part, but it was hard to imagine this virile-looking man lecturing about history to a group of high school students.

"This is a strange time to be taking a teaching job," she remarked.

"Not really. It's in between semesters. But as far as knowing anyone that might leave me her..." His shoulders lifted and fell, telling her he was just as much at a loss as she was. "I don't know anyone here or back in Texas who would do such a thing."

"Then I guess your house was just a random choice," she said thoughtfully.

Ross looked back down at the baby. She seemed to be drifting off to sleep again. He was relieved that her crying had finally stopped. No matter what Kathleen Hayes had said about it being normal, he didn't want the baby to cry. It might mean that something *was* wrong with her.

"But why?" he wondered aloud. "Why pick my house?"

Kathleen shook her head sadly as she turned toward the cabinets behind them. "People do strange things for strange reasons. I suppose the mother must have been very desperate."

"What makes you think it was the mother? It could have been the father who put her on my porch."

Kathleen grimaced. "I doubt she has a father."

Ross reached out, and Kathleen watched his finger gently stroke the baby's delicate cheek. He had big hands, she thought, with tough palms and long fingers. His skin was startlingly dark against the baby's ruddy complexion, and would be even more so against her own white skin.

The unexpected image of Ross Douglas touching Kathleen's own bare skin had her mentally shaking herself. What was she doing thinking such...erotic things? she wondered desperately. This man was a total stranger! And right now she should be thinking solely of the child.

"She has to have a father. Otherwise she wouldn't have been born," Ross reasoned.

"Biologically speaking, yes. But something tells me that if this little girl had a real father, she wouldn't have been placed on your doorstep."

"You're probably right," he conceded with a rueful twist of his lips. "And I suppose we'll find out soon enough."

Kathleen turned back to the cabinets to search for the baby bottle. Behind her, Ross realized he was still wearing his coat. Shrugging out of the damp garment, he placed it over a chair.

"Thank God, I found it," Kathleen said a minute later as she pulled the plastic bottle from a bottom shelf and held it up for him to see. "I think we would be in far worse trouble without this."

Ross joined her at the cabinet. "Maybe we could have used a rubber glove like you see in all those old movies," he said dryly. "It always seems to work."

Kathleen smiled at his suggestion, thinking they might as well try to find what humor they could in the situation. At least that was better than dwelling on the tragedy that would have occurred if Ross Douglas hadn't found the baby in time. "Well, actually, I was thinking a moment ago of an old movie where circumstances force three cowboys into taking care of an orphaned newborn."

"*The Three Godfathers*. John Wayne," he said with a grin of instant recognition.

The lazy smile caused lines to crease in his lean cheeks and sparked his gray eyes with a devilish light.

Kathleen felt her eyes drawn to his face, as though there wasn't a thing in the room to look at but him.

"You've seen it," she said.

"Yes. But let's not put axle grease on this baby of ours," he said with a low chuckle.

Kathleen was glad to see that this man was able to joke in spite of the circumstances they were in. And she was glad she could laugh along with him, because she wanted to show herself that finding this man attractive really wasn't anything to worry about.

"No. If she needs oiling, I think I can find something lighter than axle grease."

Resting his hip against the cabinet, Ross watched her punch a hole in a can of condensed milk. "Is that what the doctor said to give her?" he asked.

Kathleen pointed to the note lying on the countertop. "See for yourself."

His eyes scanned the piece of paper. "Thank God, we have something she can eat. Do you have plenty of that stuff on hand?" he asked pointing to the can.

"Plenty. I do a lot of cooking and baking and I like to be prepared," she said, finding she could not keep herself from looking at him and smiling. He returned her smile as he folded his arms across his chest.

The movement drew Kathleen's attention to the fact that he'd removed the army coat. He was wearing jeans and a dark blue crew-necked sweater with a white shirt beneath. He was built just as she'd imagined, with broad, thick shoulders and a lean, trim waist. She knew instinctively that he would be strong, as strong as her brothers, who were both as powerful as bulls.

"You don't trust me with this baby stuff, do you?" she asked more amused then resentful.

A sheepish expression crept over his face as he watched her pour a measured amount of water into the rich milk. "It's not that. I just ... want the baby to be okay."

From the corner of her eye, Kathleen saw his gaze travel over to the table where the baby lay sleeping on the folded blankets. Something inside her stirred at the tender look on his face.

"So do I. And if it will make you feel any better, I'm not a complete dimwit. As a matter of fact, I'm a schoolteacher like you. Although I'm not teaching at the present."

Ross was surprised by her admission. He'd already decided she was a wealthy woman who didn't have to work at anything. Not even at looking beautiful.

"Why not? I mean, why aren't you teaching now?"

Kathleen's eyes remained on the milk she was mixing. "My husband was killed about a year ago. It took awhile for me to gather myself back together and ... want to go back to work. By the time I did it was too late to find a junior high teaching position that was open. Maybe when the next school year starts something will be available."

He felt like a heel. But how could he have known that she'd had a husband, much less that he'd been killed?

"Sorry. That was nosy of me."

Tomorrow is the beginning of a new year, Kathleen reminded herself. She wasn't going to let thoughts of Greg drag her down anymore.

"Don't apologize. You didn't know about my late husband. Besides, friends ask me the same thing. Why aren't you teaching? Why don't you go back to teaching?"

''Does it bother you that they ask?''

Kathleen smiled wanly as she looked over at him. ''Not anymore. I'm looking forward to returning to the classroom.''

Ross didn't say anything as she went back to the task of making the formula. He only hoped she didn't teach high school. He couldn't imagine any boy over the age of fifteen being able to concentrate with her for a teacher.

''This ice storm,'' he said, ''is it something that happens very often around here?''

''It doesn't happen frequently. But we usually get a dose of it every winter.''

''Are you kidding?''

Kathleen merely smiled at his shocked expression. ''No. It's not uncommon to get stranded here on the mountain because of snow, sleet or freezing rain. Especially in January.''

''I'm from south of San Antonio. We don't have weather like this. In fact, while I was slipping and sliding up the mountainside, I was wondering why in he—heck I'd moved up here.''

''Why did you?'' She poured a portion of the prepared milk into the bottle and placed the remainder in the refrigerator.

Ross went back over to the baby. Even though she appeared to be healthy and normal, he had the uncontrollable urge to keep checking. ''A longtime friend asked me to take on the job as a favor to him. And since I was looking for a school anyway, I decided to accept the position.''

Kathleen made sure the lid and nipple were fastened tightly on the bottle before she hurried over to the microwave. ''Is it his job you're taking over?''

"No. My friend is the principal. The coach I'll be replacing was in a bad car accident and broke his leg. He'll be in a cast well into summer."

She placed the bottle in the microwave, then switched it on. While waiting for the bottle to heat, she turned around to face him. "So this is just a temporary position," she asked, "until he gets back on his feet?"

Ross shook his head. "No. This was his last year. He's retiring. That's why I bought the house. I didn't want to start out renting."

So he was planning to stay in the area, she thought. The news pleased her, though she couldn't say why. She doubted their paths as neighbors would cross once this thing with the baby and the storm were over. "It must have been hard on you to move up here on such short notice."

"Not really. I only have myself to move. And since I wasn't teaching last semester back in San Antonio, I didn't have to worry about giving notice and all that sort of thing."

If he hadn't been teaching, what had he been doing? Kathleen wondered. But she kept the question to herself. She'd already shown too much interest in the man.

Behind her the microwave dinged. Kathleen removed the bottle and tested the milk on the inner part of her arm. "Do you want to feed her?" she asked, offering the bottle to Ross.

"No," he said a bit awkwardly. "I think I'll wait and see if she can get the hang of it first."

Beneath the veil of her lashes, Kathleen gave him a long, pointed look. "If I wanted to be mean, I'd remind you of how you've continually yelled that she needed to be fed. But since I'm not that kind of person, I won't say a thing.''

An hour and a half ago Ross hadn't met this woman. So why did he feel as if he was beginning to know her already? Why did he instinctively know that she was teasing him instead of mocking him? He couldn't reason out those answers, but he did know one thing. That mischievous glint in her eye was very sexy.

''I'm glad you aren't…that kind of person,'' he said slowly, one corner of his roughly hewn mouth curving upward.

Kathleen was momentarily mesmerized by the dimple in his lean cheek, the glint of his straight white teeth, the amused light in his narrowed eyes.

''I'll just bet,'' she said, clearing her throat and moving over to the baby.

Seating herself in one of the kitchen chairs, Kathleen took the baby in her arms and offered her the bottle. After a few fumbling attempts, she managed to get the nipple into its mouth, but the baby immediately rejected it with an angry cry.

Kathleen looked up at Ross, her expression a little helpless and even more desperate. ''What am I doing wrong? Oh, Ross, what if she won't eat? What will we do?''

The baby's refusal to eat had him just as worried as Kathleen, but he tried not to let her see it. ''Don't panic. She'll eat. Just give her a minute.''

Kathleen tried again, but the baby spit out the nipple and began to cry again in earnest.

Kathleen wanted to burst into tears along with the baby. ''She doesn't want any part of it,'' she said with a frustrated groan.

"She knows you're worried and upset. Would you want to eat with somebody who was wringing her hands?"

Kathleen glared at him. "I'm not wringing my hands. I'm worried. And I've never fed a baby her very first meal! Here, you do it!"

She stood up and handed the baby over to Ross, who was instantly stunned by the reversal in their roles.

"Why do you want me to try? I don't know what to do!" he practically shouted at her.

Placing her hands on his shoulders, Kathleen pushed him down into the chair. "Neither do I. So you might as well make an attempt," she told him, then handed him the bottle.

Ross carefully positioned the baby in the crook of his arm, then crooned soft, encouraging words to her in his deep voice.

To Kathleen's amazement, the baby began to quiet down. Ross took advantage of the moment and offered her the bottle again. This time the baby got a taste of the milk and latched onto the nipple. Both adults let out a sigh of relief as the tiny girl drew greedily at the warm milk.

"I think she likes it," Kathleen declared.

Ross was aware that she'd taken up a position near his shoulder and was peering down at the baby in his arms.

"I told you she was hungry," he said.

There was such a smug, happy note to his husky voice that Kathleen just had to tilt her head around to look at him. He smiled at her, a smile that made her feel warm and glad.

"So you did, Ross. She must like you better. Or else you have that special touch," she said, smiling back at him.

Her words and her smile pleased him more than she could ever know. "I don't know about that. I just thank God she's nursing. I think she's going to be all right, don't you?"

Kathleen looked at the baby and wondered if this was how it felt to be a real parent. She would never know the answer to that, but she did know that she and this man shared a bond with this new little life. They both wanted her to be safe and protected and cared for. And so far they'd worked together to give her as much of those things as they could under the circumstances.

"Yes. I think she is. She's nursing strongly. She seems to be breathing normally. There doesn't seem to be any fever or congestion. All I can say is an angel must have sent you home just in time."

"You think I keep the company of angels, huh?"

His deep voice was tinged with wry humor, pulling Kathleen's face toward him once again. "I think you had one with you today. Before then, I couldn't say."

Ross couldn't say himself. He considered himself a good guy. At least partially good. He loved old people and children. He paid his bills, and he couldn't stand anyone who was unkind to animals. But there were thousands of people just like him. He wasn't special enough for God to have an angel looking over him. No, he somehow believed that if there had been an angel guiding him home this afternoon, it was for the baby's sake and not for Ross Douglas.

Her eyes met his and Ross felt an unfamiliar tug somewhere inside of him. "I'd like to think I have connections up in heaven," he admitted, "but it's hardly likely."

Kathleen quickly looked away from the warmth of his eyes and to the baby still nursing quietly in his arms. How long had it been since she'd looked at a man and felt like a woman? she asked herself. Years? So why was this man reminding her that it had been ages since a man had held her, ages since a man had made love to her?

She could feel Ross watching her as she stepped away from them and over to the windows that made up one wall of the room. To know that his eyes were on her made her feel warm and strange. She was desperately trying to ignore the feeling when his voice sounded behind her.

"What is it doing out there now?"

Kathleen pulled aside the curtain and peered out at the dark night. "It looks like freezing rain to me. It's really too dark on this side of the house to tell."

"Hells bells, we won't get out of here till spring thaw," he said.

His exaggeration had her glancing back over her shoulder at him. "You Texans think you've gone north if you cross the Red River."

He could see that glint back in her eyes and knew that she was teasing him again. It made Ross wonder if there was something about him that made her do it. Or did she tease all men with her words and her eyes? No. No, he didn't like to think that. He fancied the idea that he was the only one who'd seen that mysterious grin on her face.

"I know it looks bad right now," she said again. "But maybe by tomorrow the road graders will be able to push most of it off. If we're not able to drive down tomorrow, we'll surely be able to by the next day.''

Ross thought of the lone package of lunch meat on a shelf in his refrigerator. He'd intended to buy more groceries, but he'd gotten busy moving furniture and cardboard boxes filled with clothes and other bits of junk he'd collected through the years. The chore of getting in groceries had been put aside.

He watched the baby nurse and the measure of milk slowly drain out of the bottle. ''Well, I suppose I can survive on pastrami for a couple of days,'' he said with a good-natured shrug of one shoulder. ''I'm not much of a cook anyway.''

Kathleen's eyes felt glued to the man. His legs were long, she noted, the hard muscles of his thighs visible through the blue jeans. He was wearing a pair of brown cowboy boots, the high-heeled kind her brother Sam wore. She'd noticed earlier that he moved gracefully in them. When he'd paced around the kitchen with the baby in his arms, his footsteps had barely been audible on the tile floor.

Her eyes moved from his boots to glide up the length of his legs. The sitting position he'd taken had the denim jeans straining against his body in places Kathleen knew she shouldn't be looking at. But she did, anyway.

''You're not going home,'' she told him.

Chapter Four

Ross stared at her, his expression dazed. "I beg your pardon?"

Realizing just how blunt she must have sounded sent dark color spreading across Kathleen's ivory complexion.

"I only meant that it's a solid sheet of ice out there. It would be crazy for you to try to get to your house. At least for tonight, anyway. Besides, you didn't just intend to leave the baby with me, did you?"

"I hadn't had time to think that far ahead," he said, wondering how she would feel about him staying the night. She might be dead set against having a strange man in her house.

His hedging angered her. Unjustly, she supposed, but she couldn't help it. She'd been on her way to thinking that he was a man who really cared about people. She didn't like to think that she'd judged wrongly. Again.

"Oh," she said carefully, "I thought you were concerned about this baby. You certainly seemed to care awhile ago when you came to my door."

He made a frustrated sound under his breath. "I do care about her! How could you doubt that?"

Ross noticed that the baby had quit nursing. He pulled the nearly empty bottle from her mouth and motioned for Kathleen to approach. "She needs to be burped, doesn't she? I don't know how to do that, do you?"

Kathleen walked back over to him and the baby. "I think so," she said, taking the chair across from his.

Ross carefully handed her the baby. Kathleen put her on her shoulder and began to pat her back.

After a few moments passed and she didn't say anything else to him, Ross decided she must be angry with him. He also decided that he didn't like it. Whatever Kathleen Hayes thought of him, he didn't want it to be that he was an insensitive clod.

"Look, Kathleen, I want to stay here tonight and make sure you and the baby are okay. I just didn't know what *you* wanted me to do."

She stared at him as though he were crazy or close to it. "You think I'd want to be left alone with a newborn, without any means of transportation? The closest neighbor I have is you, and even if I stuck my head out the door and yelled my head off you'd be too far away to hear me." She stopped long enough to draw in a breath. "Good Lord, I've only just now stopped shaking. And we haven't even talked to the authorities about all of this yet."

Ross realized all that. Yet he was also aware of the fact that he was a man and she was a woman, and she didn't know him. At least she didn't know him well enough to share her home with him.

He looked at her. "This is your home. I didn't want to frighten you by insisting that I stay. You don't know me, and you're obviously here by yourself."

Suddenly Kathleen could see that Ross had been worried that she might have fears of being alone with him in the house. Surprisingly, the only fear Kathleen had was the fear of him not being here with her.

"I think you'll have to agree that this is an unusual circumstance. So don't worry about it. I trust you," she assured him.

Relief swept over his face. "Thank you. I assure you I'm a true Texas gentleman. You don't have a thing to worry about."

Just then the baby gave a loud, unladylike burp. Kathleen smiled down at her. "I don't want you to be a gentleman," she said to Ross. "I want you to be my friend. One that I can count on when this little girl wakes up crying in the night."

"She's going to wake up crying? I thought she'd sleep again now."

"I expect she will. For a while. But I do know that babies wake up frequently and want to eat. Haven't you ever been around a baby before?" Kathleen asked him.

Ross shook his head. "I'm an only child. Sorta."

Kathleen dabbed the milk away from the corners of the baby's mouth with a towel, then held her in the cradle of her arms. "What does 'sorta' mean?"

She was looking at the baby and didn't see the grimace on Ross's face.

"I have half brothers and sisters. Two sets of them, in fact."

Curious, she looked up at him. "Two sets?"

"Yeah. My parents split when I was ten years old. Both of them remarried and had other kids."

"Oh. I . . . see."

Ross flexed his shoulders while wondering if she really did see. He doubted it. A woman like her didn't know what it had been like as a child to be shuffled back and forth from one home to the other. He'd grown up not knowing where he belonged.

Now he avoided family contacts on either side. Both his mother and father had made their lives with someone else. They each had children of their own. Ross was the odd one out. He was a living reminder to his parents of the mistake their marriage had been.

"I doubt it, Kathleen. Something tells me you grew up in one house, with your real parents."

Kathleen was surprised by his assessment. Surprised that he'd taken that much notice of her in the first place, and surprised that he'd come up with the right deduction when he had.

"Yes, I did. On a farm not more than twenty miles from here. And I'm happy to say that my parents are together and healthy and still very much in love."

"Lucky you," he said.

Kathleen couldn't quite decide if it was wistfulness or cynicism she heard in his voice. Maybe a little bit of both. "Yes, I guess I have been," she said, then looked down at the sweet, angelic face pressed against her breast. "I wish we could say the same for this innocent baby. What in the world is she going to be able to say about her childhood when she looks back on it at my age?"

His expression quickly changed to a grim one. "We can't predict what her future is going to be. But I do know one thing. I'm going to make damn sure that the people who dumped her will never get her!''

His vehemence took Kathleen by surprise. Although it shouldn't have, she thought. Ross Douglas was a man who obviously had strong ideas about right and wrong. Just like her two brothers. And God knows, both Sam and Nick would fight till their dying day to see that justice was done. Especially where a helpless child was concerned.

"I agree. They obviously didn't want her. And she deserves to be loved. Just as every child in this world deserves to be loved."

A private little ache rushed through Kathleen's heart, compelling her to bend her head and kiss the baby's smooth cheek.

As she looked up, she realized Ross was watching her, his gray eyes filled with something that reminded Kathleen that the two of them were a man and a woman, alone.

She drew in a long breath, then let it out slowly before she spoke. "The baby seems to be fast asleep now. I think I'll take her back to the living room. The fireplace has probably made it nice and warm by now. And we need to see about calling the sheriff."

Ross was quickly on his feet. "Do you want me to carry her or can you?"

She smiled her appreciation at his offer. "I can manage her if you'll carry those blankets for me," she said, nodding toward the stack on the table.

Ross grabbed up the blankets, thinking there was nothing left for him to do but stay the night.

A quirk of a smile moved his mouth as he followed Kathleen and the baby out of the kitchen. Well, Ross, he asked himself, just how bad could it be to spend

New Year's Eve with a beautiful woman and a new-born baby?

"This feels wonderful," Ross said when the three of them entered the living room. "During the climb to your house, I didn't think I'd ever be warm again."

A long striped couch flanked by two overstuffed chairs created a sitting area in front of the fire, which was now burning brightly, filling the room with delicious heat. Kathleen placed the baby at one end of the couch and covered her with a light blanket.

"If this baby could talk, she'd probably be saying the same thing." Straightening away from the infant, she saw that Ross was standing on the hearth, his back to the fire. He was raking his fingers through the loose waves of his hair as though he were fighting fatigue.

Now that the baby was cared for and Kathleen had time to think, she was beginning to get a picture of what Ross Douglas had gone through this evening, and she had to admit she admired the man for his efforts. No doubt finding the baby had been a shock to him, Kathleen thought. Having to carry her in the freezing rain up a steep mountainside couldn't have been a picnic, either.

"You must be exhausted. Why don't you sit down and rest while I call the sheriff's department?" she suggested, heading to the phone.

He took a seat in one of the armchairs. "You're right. I am tired. That mountain out there is covered with a sheet of ice. For every foot I climbed, I slid back two."

"I can't imagine how you made it with the baby in your arms," she told him.

"Well, that wasn't as bad as trying to get up the highway in my pickup."

Kathleen had just reached for the phone, but his remarks arrested her hand in midair. "You didn't try it, did you? For heaven's sake, tell me you didn't."

Frowning, he nodded. "Now that I've calmed down enough to be able to think, I can see I was crazy to attempt it. I came close to sliding over the edge of the mountain."

The thought of him and the baby tumbling into a cold, dark ravine made her shudder with fear. "Well, thank God you didn't."

Feeling foolish even though he had no real reason to, he said, "I had to ram my truck into the ditch. I only hope it will stay there until tomorrow, or whenever I can get it out."

"If the highway workers make it up this far tonight they might push it out for you. I wouldn't worry about it," she said as she lifted the receiver to her ear. "Stranded vehicles are pretty common up here in the wintertime."

Her fingers automatically reached to punch the emergency number of the sheriff's department, then stopped as she realized there was no dial tone.

"What is the matter with this thing?" she asked aloud, clicking the receiver up and down.

"Try getting the operator," Ross suggested, seeing she wasn't having any luck.

Kathleen did, but to no avail. "Oh, brother! Now what do we do? We can't tell the authorities about any of this without a phone!"

Ross held up a calming hand. "Don't get upset. The line may start working again before long."

"But what if it doesn't? What if the sheriff thinks we kidnapped—or stole!—the baby? What if they think we deliberately avoided calling them? They might try to charge us for not reporting a felony! Oh, Ross..."

Seeing how shaken she was becoming over the whole thing, Ross went over to her. "Getting all worked up isn't going to help a thing." He took her hand in his and found her fingers cold and stiff. Instinctively, he rubbed them with his warmer ones. "And no one is going to charge us with anything. Come on now, forget it. We'll try again in a little bit."

She let out a jerky sigh as he led her over to the couch. "I know you're probably right. I guess...I don't know. Now that the urgency of caring for the baby has passed, I'm beginning to feel the shock of it all."

Ross sat down beside her on the long couch. "Believe me, I know what you're saying. I was feeling the same way when you first let me and the baby into the house." He gave her an apologetic smile. "I know I probably came on a little strong, but I'm not usually like that."

There had been a couple of times Kathleen would have taken satisfaction in slapping his face. But now that the initial crisis had passed, she understood he'd only been acting out of concern for the baby.

"I'm not usually like this, either," she told him. Realizing he was still holding her hand, she gently pulled it away. "So you're forgiven. Am I?"

He wished she hadn't withdrawn her hand. He'd liked the feel of it—the soft skin, the long, delicate fingers against his.

"There's nothing to forgive," he assured her.

"Well, now that the baby has been fed, maybe we should feed ourselves. Before you arrived I was putting a few snacks together. Have you eaten this evening?''

He looked so relieved at her question that Kathleen could hardly keep from laughing.

''To be honest with you, I'm starving,'' he admitted. ''I haven't eaten since this morning.''

''You should have said something earlier,'' she scolded, though her voice was softened by the smile on her face.

He shrugged, as though his physical comfort were of little importance. ''I didn't even realize I was hungry until now. All I could think about was the baby.''

''Me, too. But she's sleeping peacefully. So why don't you stretch out there on the couch with her, and I'll find us both something to eat.''

Ross watched Kathleen leave the room. Then, as if the woman had put some sort of hypnotic spell on him, he did as she'd suggested and stretched out lengthwise on the couch, careful to keep his boots off the cushions.

He wasn't hypnotized, Ross told himself, as he shifted his legs to a more comfortable position. He was only tired, and the events of the past couple of hours had left him rather shell-shocked. After all, it wasn't an everyday occurrence to find a baby on his doorstep. Neither was it common for a woman to have a man come bursting into her house with a newborn baby on his hands. It was no wonder they were both rattled.

His thoughts had him glancing to the end of the couch where the baby lay sleeping. Her face was red and puffy, her nose pugged, her mouth a puckered little bow. Yet when Ross looked at her, he could easily picture an endearing, freckled-face fourth grader, a beautiful young lady dressed in a prom gown.

It was strange, he thought, that he'd never felt as connected to his half brothers or sisters as he did to this child whom he'd first seen only hours ago. Maybe he should feel guilty about that. But he couldn't. This baby didn't have parents or a home. His half brothers and sisters had both.

Leaning his head against the couch, he closed his eyes and breathed a long sigh. Kathleen Gallagher Hayes. Her name swept through his mind, bringing with it strong images of the woman. She was nothing like what he'd expected her to be when she'd first let him and the baby in the front door.

Ross had expected her to be cool, proper, and probably more than a little helpless. So far she'd proven to be nothing like that, and he had to admit he was intrigued by her. And it wasn't like Ross to be intrigued by a woman. He enjoyed female company, but he wasn't a man who allowed his head to be turned a second time.

Love and marriage were for all those other guys out there. The ones who wanted the two-story house and the station-wagon-in-the-driveway kind of life. That life wasn't for Ross Douglas. He'd seen what really went on in those two-story houses, and as far as he was concerned, he'd do better without it.

Chapter Five

"I hope you don't mind leftovers."

Ross opened his eyes to see Kathleen had returned and was placing a tray of food on the low coffee table in front of him. Suddenly he didn't know which he found more tantalizing, her faint scent of jasmine or the smell of hot beef stew.

"I'll eat anything that resembles food," he said, rising to a sitting position.

She handed him a napkin and spoon. "Do you drink coffee? Or would you prefer something else? A soft drink?"

Ross realized she expected him to eat where he sat, and he glanced doubtfully at the beige-and-white sofa and the equally light-colored carpet beneath his boots. "Er—coffee is good, but my eating and this sofa may not be so good."

Kathleen began pouring two cups of coffee from an insulated pot, while the adamant shake of her head told him exactly how much she was worried about the furniture. "Don't worry about it. This is a place to live in, not to look at."

Her attitude surprised him. But then the woman had been surprising him all night, Ross realized.

She handed him the bowl of stew, then took a seat on the cushion beside him. Now that the baby wasn't distracting him, he found his senses consumed by this woman, a fact that made him feel young and foolish, and edgy. He'd never been around a woman who made him feel things without even trying, and he wasn't sure he liked it.

"So tell me," Kathleen said, "how do you usually spend New Year's Eve?"

He chuckled with wry disbelief while dipping his spoon into the bowl of stew. "Well, I don't usually go around finding abandoned babies. Thank God," he added in a more serious tone.

Kathleen took a bite of her stew, then chewed it thoughtfully before she said, "Before you arrived I was really feeling sorry for myself. Tonight my family is having a very special party. My brother Nick has just become engaged and my brother Sam arrived home this morning from his honeymoon."

"So they were expecting you. Do you think they're worried because you haven't arrived?"

Kathleen shook her head. "I talked to Nick shortly before you showed up. He ordered me not to try driving down the mountain. And when Nick orders, I mean he orders. He's a drill sergeant, you see. But he did promise to call me back."

"With the phones out, it's unlikely he'll get through to you now," Ross said.

Kathleen shrugged good-naturedly. "He's probably forgotten all about it anyway. He's so in love, he's absolutely soppy. If you know what I mean."

No, he didn't know what she meant, because Ross had never been in love. A little infatuated at times, but never in love.

"Sounds like Cupid has hit your family," he told her.

Kathleen smiled fondly. "It was about time, too. My brother Sam is a little older than me and has never been married. Nick's two years younger, but I didn't think he'd ever settle down. I'd practically given up on them." She took another bite of stew, then added, "I can say one thing, the holidays have been anything but boring this year."

Ross had barely noticed Thanksgiving. He'd spent the day alone watching football on TV. And Christmas had passed uneventfully, too. Most of his friends were in Texas. And both of his families he'd simply ignored. They each had their own children and circle of friends to celebrate the holidays with. To Ross, being alone was better than being with them and feeling like an outsider.

"I'll have to admit this tops anything that's happened to me on New Year's Eve," he said.

"I thought I was going to be spending a quiet, lonely evening alone. My family is not going to believe this!"

There was an assortment of cheese and crackers on the tray in front of him. Ross leaned forward and selected a thick slice of Muenster.

"Is going to your parents what you usually do on New Year's Eve?"

When she didn't answer promptly, Ross glanced up to see the soft smile fading from her face to leave a shadow of sadness.

The sight of it took Ross by surprise. Was she still grieving over the death of her husband? he wondered. Had they spent special, happy times together on past New Year's Eves, and did the memories still haunt her?

"To be honest with you, last New Year's went by in a fog. I don't really remember what I was doing. You see, after my husband...well, it was a long time before I could even venture out of the house." She deliberately kept her eyes away from him as she dipped her spoon into the thick stew. "But in the past, well, some New Year's Eves were spent with my parents and some of them were spent at parties given by my late husband's business associates."

"And what kind of business was that?"

As soon as the question was out, Ross knew he shouldn't have asked it. He didn't know why he had, except that he wanted to know more about this woman, and asking questions was the easiest way to go about it.

"Sorry, Kathleen. You don't have to answer that," he said quickly. "My nose is really sticking itself where it doesn't belong tonight."

Reaching for her coffee, Kathleen said, "Don't apologize. I asked you personal questions."

But she'd had a reason to, he thought. She was a woman alone, living in a secluded area. It was only natural that she'd want to know something about the man she'd allowed into her home. As for himself, Ross could only explain his interest in her as purely selfish.

Kathleen glanced at him, wondering if he had any idea what a chord he'd struck in her. One of the reasons she'd been looking forward to tonight was because for the first time in a long time, she was going to get to spend New Year's Eve with her own family, not with Greg's business cohorts. She wasn't going to have to endure their boasting and swaggering, the rooms full of tobacco smoke, the free-flowing alcohol that loosened too many tongues, the loud music and raucous laughter. No, this man couldn't know any of that.

"Greg was in the business of finding gas and oil."

"A wildcatter?"

She shook her head. "No. Actually, he was a geologist, but he ended up running the business end of things rather than doing exploration work in the field."

His expression thoughtful, Ross took a sip of his coffee. "He must have been a smart guy."

Kathleen cleared her throat and gave her bowl of stew an unnecessary stir. "Yes. Greg was well educated. He knew everything there was to know about geochemistry."

Something in her voice gave Ross the impression she was saying one thing, but feeling another. Or maybe it was just that she didn't want to discuss her late husband with him, he thought.

Either way, Ross decided he'd asked enough questions for the time being, and turned his attention back to his stew.

"I never was too much of a scientist myself," he admitted after he'd eaten a few bites. "But put a history book in my hand and I get excited."

Memories of Greg evaporated as Kathleen struggled to imagine this strong, virile man getting excited over a history book. The image left her chuckling. "I didn't know anyone got excited over history. Except maybe a college history professor, or an archaeologist."

Ross cast her a reproving glance. "Don't tell me you're one of those people who think things in the past have nothing to do with the future. Don't disappoint me like that, Kathleen."

She gave him a wry smile. "No. I'm not one of those people. Actually, I like history, especially early American. But I can't see a man like you enjoying it."

Ross wondered what she could see him enjoying. A bottle of beer and a woman hanging onto his arm? "I look that redneck, do I?"

Kathleen flushed scarlet at his question. "Of course not. I just meant that you look more like an outdoor man."

Ross placed his empty bowl on the serving tray, then, with his coffee in hand, relaxed back against the couch. Heat from the fireplace was seeping into him, making his muscles relax, his eyelids droop. "I am an outdoor man when I'm coaching baseball," he told her.

She glanced at him, her gaze quickly taking in his dark hair, thick, sooty-colored lashes partially hiding his gray eyes, the faint shadowing of beard beneath his tanned skin. He was a strong-looking man. And one who seemed totally unaware of the sensuality that exuded from his every pore. But Kathleen was aware of it. Far too aware.

"Have you always liked the game of baseball?"

After taking a sip of coffee, he answered, "Ever since I was big enough to hold a glove on my hand."

"Did you ever try to play professionally?"

His smile was lazy as he glanced over at her. "I went to the University at Austin on a baseball scholarship. Then went on to play for a minor-league team."

Ross Douglas more than liked the game, she realized. He'd been very successful at it. Her eyes continued to scan his face. "What happened? Why aren't you still playing?"

Kathleen watched his smile grow a bit wan. "The thing that happens to a lot of players—an injury. In my case it was a knee injury. Even after surgery and all sorts of therapy it couldn't hold up to the strain of the game. I was forced to retire." With a shrug he leaned forward to place his coffee cup alongside the empty bowl. "But that's all in the past now."

How sad, Kathleen thought, that his career had been cut short. But learning all about Ross Douglas's life wasn't something she should be indulging in, Kathleen told herself. She was just beginning to feel like a woman again. She had just started wanting to live again. She wasn't going to allow any man to change the course she'd set for herself. She would become an independent woman in charge of her own destiny.

"That must have been quite a blow for you. You're still very young. You could have probably played many more years. You might have even become another Nolan Ryan."

Low laughter rumbled up from his throat, making Kathleen frown with irritation.

"What's so amusing about that?" she asked.

"You comparing me to one of the greatest baseball pitchers to ever come along."

Tilting her chin up, she said, "Well, everyone has some greatness in them. As a teacher you should know that and instill it in your students."

He grinned openly. "I was laughing, Kathleen, because I played catcher."

Finding his laughter contagious, she chuckled along with him. "So he throws the ball and you catch it. I was simply trying to say that you might have become as famous as him if you'd continued to play."

He shrugged. "Maybe. I like to think so."

"Was it terribly hard for you to give up the game?" she asked, watching him closely.

"I'd be lying if I said I wasn't a bit lost at first. But I'd always planned to teach someday. So I went back to college to finish getting my teaching degree. And I can truthfully say that I'm as proud of it as I was of my baseball career."

"My daddy always said that being successful wouldn't be nearly as much fun if a person didn't experience a few failures along the way."

"Your daddy sounds like a philosopher."

Kathleen's smile was full of affection. "My daddy is a little bit of everything."

And she admired him; Ross could see it all over her face. He wished he could speak of his own father and know that his face had that same look of love and admiration. But it didn't, and he knew it. Sometimes Ross felt very guilty about that.

"Well, as far as baseball goes, teaching teenage boys how to play the game is very rewarding for me."

Kathleen's gaze traveled from his muscular thighs all the way to where his boots crossed at the ankles as she easily imagined him in a tight-fitting baseball suit. She liked his legs. Liked them far too much, she thought with a little self-disgust.

"I'm sorry that you had to retire, but I'm glad you like teaching. It's an important thing that you're doing," she said.

For long seconds, his gray eyes probed hers. "Thanks for that, Kathleen. And for saying I might have been great."

It was only a simple thank you, she told herself. So why did she feel as if he'd reached out and touched her? Why did she feel like the room was growing smaller and Ross Douglas was only a breath away?

Desperate to break the tide of her thoughts, she practically jumped to her feet and began gathering the dirty dishes. "I'm going to take these back to the kitchen."

His expression quizzical, Ross watched her leave the room. Was he imagining it, or had she suddenly grown cool with him? He couldn't think what he might have said to offend her. They'd been talking about baseball. Or had they?

The question had him muttering a silent oath. He couldn't recall a woman ever rattling him so. While a third of him conversed with her, the other two parts were soaking up the sight of her luscious body, her long, midnight black hair, her ivory white skin. It was no wonder he could remember only a small portion of what they'd been talking about.

With a snort of self-disgust, Ross left the sofa to go stand by the fireplace. At the same time he noticed another telephone sitting on a glass-topped table beside one of the chairs.

Even before he got the instrument up to his ear, Ross sensed that it was dead. Which didn't surprise him. He couldn't imagine anyone being able to work on telephone lines in such bitter weather.

Hanging up the useless phone, he walked around the room, until the sight of the sleeping baby drew him to the couch, where he squatted on his haunches for a closer look at her.

Ross still found it difficult to believe that she'd been left on his porch, that someone had actually meant for him to find her. He didn't believe it. Whoever had left the baby didn't know him. Otherwise, they would have known he didn't have the makings of a daddy, even a temporary daddy.

As though she were picking up on his doubtful thoughts, the baby squirmed and frowned. Ross reached out and gently stroked the top of her head. After a moment the squirming stopped and she made nursing movements with her mouth. Ross smiled, remembering the way she'd gone after the condensed milk. Seeing the baby eat had given him a sense of relief and joy, a feeling that had taken him by complete surprise. He didn't like to think of any child suffering, but this one, he realized, was already winding herself around his heart.

Back in the kitchen, Kathleen was certain she'd gotten herself under control. As she rinsed the dirty dishes, she tried to convince herself there was nothing different about Ross Douglas. Maybe he did happen to be young and handsome. And maybe he did have more than his share of sexuality, but that didn't mean anything to her. Moreover, any normal man would have shown the same concern over a helpless baby. He wasn't a hero. He wasn't special. He was just a man, doing what any man would have done under the circumstances. There was no reason at all for her to be feeling so drawn to him.

That idea flew straight out of Kathleen's head the moment she stepped through the opening to the living room. Ross was kneeling beside the baby, his fingertips gently brushing the top of her head. And no matter how she'd just lectured herself, her heart went soft at the look of awe and tenderness on his face.

"I hope you like German chocolate cake," she said brightly as she moved into the room.

At the sound of her voice, Ross looked up to see she'd returned. This time the tray she was carrying held a cake and dessert plates.

"I have a horrible sweet tooth. Especially for chocolate of any kind," he admitted, watching her take a seat on the floor beside the coffee table.

As she sliced into the multilayered cake, Kathleen could feel the touch of his eyes gliding over her. The subtle awareness produced a tremble in her hands, a huskiness in her voice as she spoke. "Does the baby seem all right?"

"As far as I can tell," he said, moving away from the couch and back to the fireplace. He felt restless, an unusual condition for Ross. Normally he was a laid-back person who could adapt himself to any given situation. But there was something about the quietness of this house, and the woman sitting a few steps away from him that was slowly drawing his nerves into tight little knots.

"I tried—"

"When I—"

Kathleen's laugh was short and breathy. "You go first."

"I was only going to say I tried the phone. It's still dead," he told her.

Nodding, Kathleen glanced over her shoulder at him. "I know. I tried the one in the kitchen. That's what I was going to tell you."

"We'll just have to make it without one," he said.

Kathleen turned to the table to refill Ross's coffee cup and then her own. "If it weren't for the baby, I wouldn't care that much whether it was working or not. As it is, I wish the da—darn thing was working."

Her near slip of the tongue made him smile. "Well, I'm not trying to be overly confident. I was only trying to reassure you."

At the moment, Kathleen wasn't quite sure what was making her need reassurance, the baby or Ross Douglas. If the baby should need more attention than she or Ross knew how to give, having a phone would be a big help. In fact, if the phone was working, she might even be able to manage caring for the baby on her own, and not have to rely on Ross Douglas.

With him in his own house, she wouldn't have to deal with the awkward tension she felt every time he looked at her. She wouldn't have to think about the carnal urgings she felt every time she looked at him!

But the phone wasn't working, she quickly reminded herself, and she needed him to stay for the baby's sake. And even if the phone was working, would she really want him to leave?

Carrying a slice of cake and a cup of coffee over to him, she had to admit that she was beginning to like the company, and the man.

"I just wish I could feel as calm as you do about the situation," she said with a sigh.

Kathleen believed he was calm? He must be quite an actor, Ross thought. Otherwise, she could see that every time she got within five feet of him, his senses crackled like electricity jumping from one frazzled wire to another.

Murmuring his thanks, he took the dessert plate from her. "Did you bake this?"

"Yes. This morning. I made it for the party tonight."

"Your brothers are probably missing this." Lifting a bite to his mouth, he forced his eyes to shift away from her.

Kathleen laughed softly as she went back to her seat on the floor. "If you knew my mother, you would know the place will be running over with food. Besides, I really doubt Sam or Nick will be thinking about food tonight."

So love and marriage had put her brothers on a cloud, Ross thought with grim amusement. It probably wouldn't be long before both of the poor saps hit the ground with a thud.

But when Ross spoke again he was careful to keep that opinion to himself. "You said that Nick was a drill sergeant. What does your other brother do?"

"He's a farmer. In fact, now that my father has retired, Sam has taken over the Gallagher farm."

"Sounds like both of your brothers are smart, ambitious men."

"Handsome, too. To tell you the truth, I don't know how either of them stayed bachelors for as long as they did."

Ross didn't know how old her brothers were or how long they'd avoided marriage, but so far he'd found it very easy to stay away from the altar. He never allowed any relationship go beyond two or three dates, and if the woman of the moment persisted, he'd find a reason to back away.

"How did they manage?" he asked.

Kathleen shook back her long hair as she thought about his question. "Actually, Sam's true love was in Africa for four years. She was a relief worker in Ethiopia, a whole story in itself. But it wasn't until she came home this Thanksgiving that they reconciled their differences and realized they were both madly in love." She smiled at the memory, then glanced over to see that Ross was watching her intently. She felt herself blush like an innocent teenager.

"As for Nick," she went on, trying with all her might not to be affected by this man and his cool gray eyes, "it's still difficult for me to believe he's headed for the altar. He's always loved women as much as he loves to bark orders. But—" she shrugged as a wistful smile transformed her features "—Allison seems to have changed all that. I've never seen him so dotty over a woman. Of course, you'd probably be dotty over her, too, if you could see her."

"Pretty, huh?"

"Exquisite. Strawberry blond hair below her shoulders. Skin like milk and one of those tiny waists that most women have to kill themselves in a gym for. But not Allison. Hers is natural. And Olivia is a dream, too. She and I were best friends in college and I always felt dowdy compared to her."

Ross smiled to himself as he watched her cut a sliver of cake for herself. He could have told Kathleen Gallagher Hayes that she had nothing to worry about in the looks department. He couldn't imagine anyone looking more beautiful than she did at this moment, sitting on the floor, her image bathed in fire glow.

"So you like both of them?"

"Oh, I love them. They're both like my sisters. Of course, I've known Olivia for years, but it didn't take me long to get close to Allison. As a matter of fact, we were friends before Nick was ever introduced to her. She's a strong young woman. There's not many of them out there who could raise a child alone, without help from anyone, the way Allison has."

Ross was silently speculating over Kathleen's remarks when she shifted around to face him.

"She's an unwed mother," Kathleen felt compelled to add. "So you see, I admire her as well as love her."

"What happened to the father?"

Her lips pursed ruefully. "You're being kind, calling him a father. In my dictionary, he's described by a totally different term. You'll find it listed in the *B*s."

One thing was certain about Kathleen Hayes, he concluded; she certainly wasn't shy about voicing her opinions. "I take it he didn't live up to his responsibilities?"

Kathleen shook her head as she sipped her coffee. "He skipped out as soon as he discovered she was pregnant. Allison's own father wasn't any better. He washed his hands of her, too. Because she'd behaved immorally, or so Allison says. Frankly, I believe the old man just didn't want to be bothered with helping her."

"Sounds like your future sister-in-law has had some tough knocks," Ross said.

Kathleen nodded, then her features suddenly brightened with a smile. "Well, I can safely say that's over with. Nick adores her and Allison appears to worship him. I can't see them having anything but a wonderful life ahead of them.''

It was obvious to Ross that Kathleen was a romantic. Apparently the loss of her husband hadn't sullied her belief that love and marriage always equaled happiness.

"So when did Sam get married? Obviously sometime between Thanksgiving and now."

She groaned good-naturedly. "We had a big wedding at the farmhouse on Christmas Eve. I didn't know if we were going to live through it and Christmas together. On top of that, Nick and Allison didn't meet until two days before Christmas. Keeping up with this?'' she asked with a chuckle.

He shook his head wryly. "Must have been instant combustion.''

"Instant," she agreed. "They became engaged before Sam and Olivia returned from their honeymoon in Telluride.''

His brows lifted at this news. "I'd call that a cold honeymoon.''

Kathleen couldn't know her low laughter shivered over Ross's skin. He drew in a long breath and told himself to quit looking at her. But his eyes refused to obey. They fastened on her cherry-colored lips, which had him instantly wondering what it would be like to taste them instead of the chocolate cake he was eating.

"I doubt it," she said. "When you're madly in love you don't get cold. Or didn't you know that?''

Chapter Six

That teasing lilt was back in her voice, but the little smile on her mouth was definitely an enigma, making him unable to decide if her question was a challenge or an invitation. He liked to think the latter. But thinking like that had gotten Ross into trouble more than once in his life.

His gaze dropped from hers, but not before Kathleen saw a slow grin spread across his face. He couldn't know how boyishly endearing he was to her at that moment.

"I guess it's true that a man can learn something everyday," he said.

Kathleen had to struggle to keep from laughing aloud. Who was he kidding? she wondered. A man who looked like him had to have had women in his past. More than likely several of them.

Kathleen, she silently scolded herself, even if the man has had women in his past doesn't necessarily mean he's been in love. Greg had clearly and painfully proven that to her. A man was usually in lust, not in love.

"Well," she said, her voice suddenly losing its warmth, "then I guess you consider yourself lucky."

Ross supposed he did think himself lucky for eluding that condition called love, so why did it bother him to admit it to this woman?

"Are you trying to ask me if I've ever been on a honeymoon?"

His bluntness brought pink color to her cheeks, but she continued to meet his gaze in spite of it. "No. I don't have to ask. You have that unattached look."

Instinctively Ross glanced at himself, as if there was something on the outside that he'd failed to see. "What is it about me that doesn't look attached?" he asked, his expression quizzical.

Kathleen had never intended for their conversation to stray this far, but now that it had, she decided the best thing to do was handle it lightly. Giving him a smile, she said, "Just about everything."

To know that she'd looked at him that closely, even in a dispassionate way, heated his blood with sexual thoughts. "Well, I haven't been married. I came close once. Or at least I thought the relationship was heading toward marriage. But it didn't happen," he said, thinking about the woman who'd turned her back on him once she'd learned his baseball career had ended. "That experience opened my eyes," he went on. "I don't ever want to permanently attach myself to a woman. By marrying her or any other way," he added for good measure.

So he'd had a broken relationship, too, she silently mused. It was no wonder that he'd wanted to leave

Texas and start a fresh life in a new place. "I know what you mean," she told him with unwavering certainty. "Because I don't want to be married, either."

She rose to her feet and moved to the baby. Ross watched her bend over the child and brush her fingers over her brow. "I don't understand," he felt compelled to say. "You seem ecstatic about your brothers getting married."

Satisfied that the baby was sleeping normally with quiet, regular breathing, Kathleen straightened, then looked over her shoulder at Ross Douglas.

"I am ecstatic. I'm thrilled to high heaven for them. And Olivia, that dear woman, deserves every bit of happiness my brother Sam can give her."

"Hmm. I guess I'm missing something, or I just don't get it," Ross told her. "You're obviously thrilled about your brothers getting married, and you believe they'll both be happy. But you don't want marriage for yourself."

"That's right. See, you didn't miss a thing." She walked across the room to the windows and parted the drapes with her hand.

Ross stared at her, still not quite sure he'd heard her right. Although he didn't know why her response had shocked him so. Not every woman wanted to be married. Many of them had careers to think of, and others merely valued their independence, like he did. So why did it surprise him to hear that Kathleen Hayes was one of those women?

Because she was obviously a romantic. Her eyes had a special glow when she'd talked about her brothers marrying the women they loved. It only seemed natural that she would want the same thing for herself— eventually.

Kathleen continued to look out the window. The sleet had turned to snow. Already the ground was covered with a thick white carpet. If the weather had been anything other than this, she mused, she would have been partying with her family tonight. And more than likely she would never have met Ross Douglas. She would have read about the baby being found on his porch in the morning newspaper. Was fate playing some sort of trick on her? Had it sent the ice and snow just so she would be home tonight?

She glanced around to see he was watching her, his expression quiet and contemplative. "I've been married once," she told him. "And I don't believe I could find happiness in marriage again."

Ross realized there were all sorts of things he could read from her words. But he quickly told himself to forget them. Kathleen Hayes's personal life was really none of his business. In fact, it would be a big relief if he could walk out the door right now and pretend he'd never met the woman. She was trouble. He could feel it as easily as he felt the heat from the fireplace. But there was the baby to think about. He didn't want to leave her, and he didn't want to leave Kathleen alone with her.

"I guess losing a spouse would disillusion a person," he said.

He couldn't know how disillusioned, she thought. Because Ross Douglas didn't know that she'd lost her husband long before the accident that had taken his life.

"He was killed in weather like this," she found herself telling him. "In a plane over the Boston Mountains. Greg was a good pilot. But apparently the flight instruments failed and the snow was so heavy there was no visibility."

Ross's eyes fell from her pained expression to the toes of his boots. "I've never lost anyone close to me," he said quietly, "but then there's not too many people that want to be close to me."

Rubbing her arms to chase away the chill, Kathleen moved from the window and came to stand a few steps away from him. "I really doubt that. With two sets of families you must have lots of close relatives."

With a wry twist to his mouth he said, "Let's just say I have relatives. The closeness part...I'd call questionable."

He leaned forward and placed his empty dishes on the coffee table. "While you were in the kitchen, I was thinking about the baby."

"What about her?"

"She needs a name. Or are we just going to keep calling her 'the baby'?"

Kathleen met his sidelong glance with a questioning one. "We don't have a right to name her. Do we?"

"Who has a better right? At the moment we're her parents. Besides, I'm not talking about a legal name. We can consider it our right to name her. For the time being."

Kathleen's eyes slipped away from his face and over to the baby, who'd started to squirm and wake. "Well, I suppose it wouldn't hurt. If the authorities had her they'd probably tag her Baby Doe or something equally awful."

"You're right. So what should we call her?"

A smile softened Kathleen's features as she took a seat beside the newborn baby. "I don't know. Naming a child is something I've never done."

Ross looked down at both of them. "Neither have I," he admitted. "Don't people usually name babies after their relatives?"

"Some do. I was named after my aunt on my mother's side. What about you?"

"My paternal grandfather. He was a World War 1 veteran and hell with the ladies."

Kathleen could hear a hint of fondness in his voice. Looking up at him, she said, "I take it he was one relative you were close to."

Ross nodded. "Yeah. He lived to be ninety. He drank a cup of hot water every morning and read the Bible every evening after supper. And he never went to bed without having a shot of bourbon. For medicinal purposes, of course."

"Oh. Of course," Kathleen said with a knowing laugh.

"Well, it's a cinch our little gal doesn't have any relatives to be named after—at least that we know of."

Kathleen studied the tight grimace on his face. "I take it you're not a forgiving man."

His eyes widened as he realized she *expected* him to be forgiving. "Let's put it this way. I find it very hard to understand how someone could leave a baby out in the cold."

"I understand how you feel. I feel the same way. Even though I'm trying not to."

He narrowed his eyes. "Why are you trying not to?"

Kathleen shrugged as she tried to come up with a reason why someone would leave a baby on a doorstep. "It's not good to be judgmental of other people. Especially when we don't know anything about the circumstances."

His sardonic expression disappeared as he considered Kathleen's words.

"You're obviously a kind-hearted woman. But you are right about being judgmental. I don't want to condemn whoever left the baby. But I would like to know why."

He came over to the couch and squatted down beside them.

Kathleen allowed herself a moment to study him at close range. With his head bent down toward the baby, she could see that his dark hair had dried after his icy trek up the mountain. For the most part it was cut short, except for the top, which fell to one side of his forehead in undisciplined waves. His skin was smooth, but coarsely textured, and a startling contrast against his white teeth, although she supposed he'd lose the dark tan now that he'd moved north.

"So, back to the baby," she said, in an effort to halt her straying thoughts. "Do you have a name in mind for her?"

One of his shoulders lifted, then fell as his eyes drifted down to the baby's face. "Not really. Every time I look at her I keep thinking how shocked I felt when I discovered her in that box."

"She certainly arrived under unusual circumstances. Not to mention in one of the worst ice storms I can remember."

"Hmm. Forget the ice and snow. This little girl created a storm all by herself. She just doesn't know it yet."

"Then maybe we should call her Stormy," Kathleen suggested, her gaze encompassing both him and the baby.

Ross looked at Kathleen, then a grin spread slowly across his face. "Yeah. Stormy. I like that." He glanced down at the baby. "What about you, little one?"

At the sound of his voice, the baby's face scrunched up and grew even redder. In a matter of seconds she was crying lustily.

"Good Lord, she must hate the name," Ross said with a faint chuckle.

Kathleen pulled back the blanket and quickly discovered that the new little Stormy needed changing. "She doesn't understand a thing you're saying. Right now she doesn't care what you call her. She's trying to tell you to change her diaper."

"Me?" Ross asked with amazement. "What about you? You're the mother here."

"And you're the father. Nowadays fathers change diapers, too."

"Whoa, now," he said, thrusting his palms up. "You can't expect me to be an instant father, and— and know about these things."

"Why not?" Kathleen asked, finding his reluctance more amusing than anything. "You expected me to know about these things."

He cleared his throat. "Well, yes. But that's different. You're a woman. This kind of stuff comes natural to you."

Dimples appeared on either side of her mouth as she tried to hold back a smile. "I'm certain it will come naturally to you, too. Just watch her while I go get a diaper from the kitchen."

Ross rose so quickly to a standing position that his knees made a loud popping noise.

"My catcher's knees," he explained, seeing Kathleen's quizzical look. "They're getting stiff. Uh, let me go get the diaper for you."

He left the room in a quick stride. Kathleen laughed softly, then said to the fussy baby, "Men won't always run from you, Stormy. When you're all grown up, you'll be so pretty they'll be running to you. As far as that goes, I've got a daddy and two brothers you could easily wind around your finger right now."

The thought of her family made the smile fade from Kathleen's lips. She'd used to dream of giving her parents a grandchild, her brothers a niece or a nephew. These past few years she'd had to face the fact that those dreams would never come true. She'd thought she had adjusted to the reality of being childless. Until now. Having this newborn baby in her home and in her arms was bringing all the old yearnings back to her.

"Here. I brought the whole stack."

Kathleen looked around to see that Ross had returned with the diapers. Realizing her eyes had misted over, she blinked them and did her best to smile.

"Thank you," she said taking one of the squares of sheeting. "Did the trip to the kitchen stretch your legs?"

"My legs?"

"You know. The problem with your knees," she reminded him. "I hope you didn't hurt your injured knee when you were climbing the mountain."

He took a seat in the nearby chair that sat at an angle to her and the baby. "Oh, no," he said, oddly touched by her concern for him. "The knee is fine. It's just that from the time I was eight years old I spent every summer in a squatting position. Sometimes the knees balk when I tell them to straighten out.''

She spread the sheeting out on the cushion to her right and folded it into a small rectangle. ''I've often wondered what keeps my brother Nick's legs going. He does so much marching and running with the troops.'' She glanced over at him, then smiled impishly. ''Are you watching this closely? Next time it's going to be your turn.''

From the corner of her eye, Kathleen could see Ross crossing his legs at the ankles and resting his head against the back of the chair.

''The only diaper I ever changed was the kind with tapes on it. I couldn't pin that thing. I'd stick her.''

Kathleen removed the damp towel from the baby, then slipped the dry diaper beneath her bottom. ''No, you won't,'' she said, then motioned for him to come close. ''Here, I'll show you.''

Ross went over and squatted beside Kathleen and the baby. ''Are you sure I'm going to need to learn how to do this?''

Kathleen turned her head to find his face was dangerously close to hers. And when their eyes collided, her heart reacted with a strange little thump that quickly turned into a wild gallop.

''We, uh, don't know how long the snow and ice will last. For all we know we may have to be her parents for several days.''

Several days? Ross didn't know if he could survive being around this woman for several days. She already had him thinking things he shouldn't be thinking, and wanting to do things he shouldn't want to be doing.

"I don't know anything about being a daddy," he said, his eyes skimming over her pale features. She had thick black lashes that were long enough to be false, but Ross knew they weren't. Everything about this woman was genuine and beautiful.

Her full lips curved into a wan smile. "I don't know how to be a mother, either. I guess we can learn together."

"Let's hope we do it right," he said, his eyes dropping to the curve of her moist lips.

Suddenly breathless, Kathleen turned back to the baby. "See," she said, hoping her voice didn't betray her runaway heart. "You put your fingers between the baby and the diaper, then you use your other hand to pin with. That way if you stick anything, it will be yourself."

She pinned one side of the diaper to show him how, leaving the other side. He looked at her skeptically as she held the pin out to him.

"You must have been hell on wheels in the classroom. I'll bet your students learned a lot. Even the ones that didn't want to," he said wryly, taking the pin from her fingers.

"I like to think they did."

Ross reached for the diaper, and from the corner of his eye he could see Kathleen smile. His attempts to help care for the baby obviously pleased her, and that gave Ross a strange feeling of satisfaction. What man alive wouldn't like to believe he could please a beautiful woman like Kathleen? he asked himself. But to be doing it by pinning a diaper on a baby was certainly a new one for Ross.

Kathleen watched his fumbling attempts for a moment before she reached for his left hand. "Put your thumb here, and three fingers back here," she said, positioning them on the piece of white cloth. "Now lap this over with your other hand, hold it down with this thumb, and pin."

Ross did as she instructed, but his mind wasn't on the job. She was so close to him that her scent filled his nostrils, and the gentle touch of her hand on his only had him thinking of how soft and smooth the rest of her must feel.

"There you are," Kathleen told him. "I knew you could do it. You're going to be a natural."

"You think so?" he asked, his eyes back on her face.

Even though the job was finished, Kathleen realized her fingers were still curved around his, and for one wild second, she wanted to tighten her hold on him, to lean forward and taste his lips.

What was she thinking? Why was she feeling these things? The questions shot fear into her, one that had nothing to do with the ice storm or the baby. She quickly jumped to her feet.

"I think...uh, if you'll watch the baby, I'll turn on the TV and see if we can get a weather forecast."

With a puzzled frown, Ross watched her cross the room and switch on a large set that was built into an entertainment center. He'd felt for certain that she'd been about to say something else. He'd even thought for one split second that she might kiss him.

Ross, have you totally lost your mind? he asked himself. Well, maybe she hadn't been about to kiss him, he argued. Maybe she'd been going to let him kiss her. That's just as crazy, Ross, he fiercely told himself. Forget it. Forget about kissing. Think about the storm, the baby, anything but Kathleen Hayes.

Chapter Seven

The TV weatherman predicted snow through the remainder of the night, with clearing skies in the morning and high temperatures for tomorrow ranging in the twenties.

When the station broke for a commercial, Ross looked at Kathleen, who'd taken a seat on the floor by the fireplace.

"What kind of shape will that leave us in?" he wanted to know. "If it snows all night, we might not be able to get to the highway, much less to the city."

Kathleen glanced away from the TV screen and over to where Ross sat closely watching the baby. Even though Stormy was asleep, it was obvious that he wanted to be near her, as though somehow their trek together through the snow had bonded him to her.

"I don't know. But we do have a good highway department and they'll be out working round the clock, so that if people are stranded it won't be for long."

Kathleen rose to her feet and went over to the phone. Lifting the receiver to her ear, she found no dial tone, and she wondered what her family would say when she was finally able to reach them with the news of little Stormy. It was going to be a shock, to say the least.

"It's still dead," she told Ross, seeing the expectant look on his face.

Groaning, Ross passed a tired hand over his face. "What time is it, anyway?"

Kathleen pushed back the sleeve of her sweater to glance at her wristwatch. "Oh, my! It's almost twelve. The new year is almost here!"

The approaching midnight hour suddenly reminded her of the champagne she'd left chilling in the refrigerator. "We've got to celebrate!" she said, quickly heading out of the room. "I'll be right back."

Ross was still on the couch with the baby when Kathleen returned, but he got to his feet the moment he saw she was carrying a bottle of champagne and two long-stemmed glasses.

"When you say celebrate, you really mean celebrate," he said.

She laughed at the surprised look on his face. "Actually, I'd bought this for Nick and Allison. But what the heck. If they can't enjoy it, we might as well."

She placed the glasses on the coffee table, then handed the bottle to Ross. "Would you do the honors of opening it?"

"Sure. But maybe we'd better move away from the baby. I don't want to spray her with champagne after all she's been through tonight."

At the other end of the room there was a love seat positioned in front of the TV, and Kathleen motioned to it. "Let's go over there. Maybe one of the stations will be having a countdown to midnight."

While Ross worked the cork in the champagne bottle, Kathleen switched television channels.

"Oh, look, this one is showing the scene at Times Square in New York City!"

She'd barely gotten the words out when the cork popped and the pale gold liquid erupted from the bottle. Laughing, she held the glasses out to Ross, who managed to fill them without losing too much onto the floor.

"I wasn't expecting to have champagne tonight," he told her, his gray eyes warm on her smiling face. "Especially not with a beautiful woman."

Her green eyes sparkled back at him. "Oh, don't tell me you're a flatterer, along with being a savior, too."

A touch of color swept across his dark face. He didn't know why he'd let that last little bit slip. But at the moment he didn't care. Kathleen was beautiful, and the way she smiled was like no other woman had ever smiled at him. "I'm hardly a savior. Just a man who found a baby."

Kathleen shook her head. "You're being too modest. And as for expecting things, I never expected to see a strange man and a baby in my house tonight!"

And he'd never expected to find a woman like her in this house, or any other place. But he kept the thought to himself. "So are we going to make a toast?" he asked.

"Of course! We have a wonderful reason to make a toast. To our new little Stormy. She wasn't born on New Year's Day, but very close to it." Kathleen softly clinked her glass against his. "And if it weren't for you, Ross, she wouldn't be starting life in this new year. God bless you for saving her life," she whispered, her eyes suddenly brimming with tears.

His eyes were riveted on her face as pride, joy, desire all rushed through him, bubbling and fizzing like the champagne in his glass. Never in his life had Ross felt like he did at this moment. And before he knew what he was doing, he'd reached out and pulled her against him.

"Happy New Year, Kathleen Gallagher Hayes," he whispered before bringing his lips down on hers.

Kathleen didn't know which stunned her more, the fact that he was kissing her, or the fact that it felt so good.

But as the kiss went on, both thoughts flew off into oblivion. Because he'd gone beyond just kissing her. He was tasting her, luring her, silently asking her to kiss him back. And Kathleen found it impossible to refuse him. For long moments, she stood on tiptoe and kissed him with a passion she'd never expected to feel.

The moment he finally lifted his mouth away from hers, she whispered breathlessly, "Happy New Year, Ross Douglas."

Ross looked down at her and knew he couldn't have been more intoxicated than if he'd just drunk a whole bottle of champagne.

"I think it's midnight," he said unsteadily.

Kathleen glanced at the TV, where people were shouting and kissing and singing "Auld Lang Syne." "Yes, an old year is gone and a new one begins. Shall we drink to it?"

Ross would rather kiss to it, but he wasn't going to act on his impulses again. One taste of her had been like a wham in the head with a sledgehammer, and

Ross wasn't a man who went around deliberately asking to be hurt.

"Sure," he said, bringing his glass up to his lips. "To the new year and to Stormy."

Grateful for the diversion, Kathleen took a long sip of the bubbly liquid, then another.

She didn't know what was happening to her, she thought, as she sank weak-kneed to the love seat. She'd never experienced such a strange mixture of feelings in her life. She was happy and excited, scared and shaky. And even more, she felt drawn to Ross, connected to a man she'd never seen until tonight. It was all happening too fast, she thought. Her emotions were whirling around inside her like a ray of multicolored lights.

"Would you like some more?"

She glanced up to see that Ross was holding up the champagne. "Er, no, one glass is enough for me. I don't want my senses to be dulled. Stormy might wake up and need another bottle."

He could sense she was drawing away from him. Probably because she was regretting that kiss. Well, he was regretting it, too. Because Ross knew that one kiss was going to be hell to forget. "It's getting late, and you must be exhausted. Why don't you go to bed?" he suggested. "I'll sit up with the baby. I know what to do now. I think."

Kathleen quickly shook her head. "No. I couldn't leave you with her. You go to bed. There're four bedrooms down the hall—just take your pick, except for the last one on the right. That one is mine."

Ross shook his head in turn. "I couldn't. But you suit yourself."

Even though Kathleen was exhausted, she knew if she went to bed, she wouldn't be able to sleep a wink. Not with him and the baby in here. And definitely not with everything that was going on in her head.

She finished her champagne, then carried her empty glass over to the coffee table. Stormy was still asleep, her tiny little fist drawn up to her mouth. With a surge of protectiveness, Kathleen tucked the blanket closer, then whispered, "Good night, little one. Ross and I will be here to watch over you."

Kathleen didn't know what woke her first, the baby's cries or the ringing of the telephone. But by the time she managed to open her eyes and push herself to a sitting position, Ross had picked up Stormy and was carrying her toward the kitchen.

"You get the phone. I'll heat her bottle," Ross tossed over his shoulder.

Kathleen hurried over to the phone, half afraid the caller would hang up and she'd lose all connection to the outside world.

"Hello."

"Good morning, Kathleen. How are things on the mountain?"

"Sam! Oh, Sam, it's so good to hear your voice. You're not going to believe what's happened!" She quickly began to relate the whole story, finally ending with, "Ross has just now taken her to the kitchen to feed her."

"Ross? You mean the man is there with you now? You let a strange man you don't even know spend the night in your house? Kathleen, have you gone crazy or what? You don't know where he found this baby! He could have kidnapped it, for heaven's sake!"

How strange it sounded for her brother to be saying she didn't know Ross. He already seemed so much a part of her. But Sam wouldn't understand that. Sam took a slow approach with everything. "Sure, Sam, he probably did, just so he could bring it up here to me," she said dryly.

Her brother let out a sigh of resignation. "I guess you're right, sis. But I thank God we didn't know about this last night, or I would have been worried."

"Of course I'm right. Besides, Ross is my neighbor. He's moved into the old Mabry place down the road from here. Remember?"

"Yes, I remember. So what are you going to do now?"

"Well, we've tried to call the authorities to report everything, but my phone has been dead. I guess now that we can do that, we'll see what they have to say."

"Yes, do that, pronto. And Kathleen, maybe you'd better get in touch with Parker Montgomery. You might need some legal advice—you never know about these things."

"You're right," Kathleen said, shoving her tousled hair off her forehead. "I'll call him first. Once we talk to the authorities and get things straightened away, I'll call you back and let you know what's happening."

"Well, don't keep us waiting long. As soon as I get off the phone and tell this story, the whole house is going to be in an uproar."

Kathleen could very well imagine. "I'll call as soon as I can," she promised, then hung up and hurried out to the kitchen.

She found Ross still feeding the baby. There were lines of fatigue on his face, but he looked more rested than he had last night after midnight, when he'd fallen asleep on the floor by the fireplace.

Rather than wake him, Kathleen had covered him up with blankets, then had lain down on the couch with the baby. It was the last thing she remembered before waking up this morning.

"Who was that calling at this hour? It's only five o'clock!"

Kathleen went straight to the coffeemaker and began filling it with cold water. "It was my brother Sam. I told you he's a farmer. Five o'clock in the morning is late to him."

Ross's eyes ran up and down the length of her. As he noticed her feet, he began to smile. "I see you finally took your high heels off."

Groaning, she looked down at her stockinged feet, then back up at him. She knew she probably looked horrible. Her hair was tumbled and tangled, her face without makeup. "I decided the party was over. Want some breakfast? Looks like Stormy is getting hers."

"She was definitely hungry. And so am I. But maybe we'd better talk with the police before we do anything else."

She nodded as she quickly finished putting the coffee makings together. "You're right. While the coffee drips, we'll make the call."

For the next few minutes Ross related his part of the story, then Kathleen took the phone and related hers. When they were finally allowed to hang up, Kathleen said, "They didn't act nearly as surprised about this whole thing as I thought they would."

"They're police officers. They're used to hearing and seeing shocking things."

"I guess you're right, but I wish we didn't have to go down to the station. We've already told them everything we know."

Ross shrugged as he took a seat at the kitchen table. "They do need to see the baby, so they'll know we haven't just fabricated this whole thing. And I'm sure they'll probably want us to hand her over to them."

Kathleen stared at him in horror. "Are you crazy? I'm not handing Stormy over to them!"

Ross looked across the table at her and was amazed to see that she was visibly shaking. "What do you mean?" he asked. "Right now she's an orphan. A ward of the court."

Kathleen shook her head vehemently. "No! I don't want her to be a ward of the court. They'll send her off to some crowded orphanage, or to some foster parents she won't even know! She's just been born, Ross, and all she knows is you and me. It would be better if we could keep her, for a few days at least. Don't you think so?"

If we could keep her. Ross couldn't help but notice how she included him, as though he were going to continue to be a part of this whole thing.

Before he'd fallen asleep last night, Ross had told himself that the best thing he could do was get the baby to the right authorities, and then back away and go on about his own business. Forget Stormy and forget Kathleen. But in the light of day, with the now-familiar weight of that little being in his arms, he knew deep down that he didn't want to hand the baby over any more than Kathleen did.

Dear Lord, Ross, you're thinking with your heart now, and that kind of thinking will get you into trouble. You know that! "I don't know, Kathleen. In the case of a child, I don't think you can apply the rule of Finders, Keepers.''

Kathleen suddenly snapped her fingers and jumped to her feet. ''I haven't called Parker yet. He can fix things. He'll know exactly what to do.''

''Who's Parker?''

''Parker Montgomery. He's an old friend of mine, who also happens to be a lawyer. He handled all my legal affairs when Greg was killed,'' she told him as she headed for the phone on the breakfast bar. Quickly she began punching out his number. ''And he has friends in high places.'' She glanced over her shoulder at him. ''So keep your fingers crossed. Stormy isn't going to become a Baby Jane Doe yet.''

By noon the sun was shining brightly and the road crew had managed to clear the highway enough to make it passable. Ross got his pickup out of the ditch, then stopped by his house long enough to take a shower and change into clean clothes. By the time he returned to Kathleen's house, she had herself and the baby ready to go into Fort Smith and the police station.

She'd changed into a pleated corduroy skirt and matching long-sleeved shirt. The outfit showed off her small waist and the red color looked luscious against her dark hair. She was wearing red lipstick, too, Ross noticed. And he found he was having trouble keeping his eyes off her. Especially her lips, which seemed to be smiling at him more often than not.

''I'm glad to see you made it back in one piece. Is the highway clear enough to make it down safely?'' she asked.

FIND OUT **INSTANTLY** IF YO
UP TO 5 FREE GIFTS IN T

CARNIVAL W

▼ SCRATCH-OFF GAME

Scratch off ALL 3 gold areas

YES! I have scratched off the 3 Gold Areas above
gifts for which I qualify. I understand I am under
any books, as explained on the opposite page.

NAME

ADDRESS

CITY   STATE

PLAY THE

CARNIVAL WHEEL

GAME . . .

GET AS MANY AS FIVE GIFTS FREE!

PLAY FOR FREE! NO PURCHASE NECESSARY!

HO

1. W
off the
Carniv
or mor
novels
depend
beneat

2. R
Wheel
ately s
you qu

3. T
otherw
you 6
enjoy,
availa
them
decide
$1.99
applic
the co
to cov
stores

4. Y
guara
any ti
or by
cost.
gift r

No
No

* Term
notic
©19

"There's still a lot of snow in places, but the road crew has spread sand on it. Plus there's traffic moving now, so it must be passable," he told her.

"Maybe we should take my car. It has front-wheel drive," she suggested. "I certainly won't mind, if you promise to drive. I'm not very good on ice."

He gave her a wry grin. "You think I am? If you'd seen me last night, you wouldn't be asking me to get behind the wheel of your car."

She fished the keys out of her purse and tossed them to him anyway. "I trust you. I'll bring Stormy out when I think the car has had time to warm up."

They left the house a few minutes later. Ross wasn't that keen on driving. One wrong slip and he could cause Kathleen or the baby to be hurt, and that thought kept a knot of fear in his stomach as he slowly maneuvered the car down the winding highway. On the other hand, Kathleen seemed to be completely relaxed, absorbed with the beauty of the snow and the baby in her lap.

"I wish I'd had something to dress Stormy in," she told Ross, after they'd traveled a few miles. "The only thing I could find was a shrunken T-shirt of mine. It was far too large, but I thought it would serve the purpose of a gown."

"We'll get something for her when we're finished at the police station," Ross told her as he carefully steered the car over large patches of snow and ice.

"I know I'm not supposed to be holding her in my lap while we're traveling. I should have strapped her into a car seat." She tapped her finger thoughtfully against her chin. "Maybe I should get one of those, too. And some bottles and diapers." She looked over at Ross. "Gosh, I never realized how many things a newborn needs!"

Ross knew he should probably remind her that she was going to have the baby with her for only a brief time, if any time at all. But he couldn't bring himself to. He could see the way she was cuddling the baby to her breast, the tender love on her face each time she looked at it. She didn't want to give her up now, and he was beginning to doubt that she ever would.

Kathleen's lawyer met them at the police station. He was somewhere around forty, Ross figured, with a head of sandy-colored hair and brown eyes that kept sizing Ross up and smiling at Kathleen.

Ross didn't know whether he liked the man or not, but Kathleen seemed to trust him implicitly, so he figured that was all that really mattered.

Once the interview with the police was over, the lawyer walked with the three of them out to the parking lot.

"You don't have anything to worry about," he told Kathleen. "I've already talked with Judge Lawton and he's agreed to let you have temporary custody until a suitable foster home can be found for her."

Kathleen cringed inwardly. "And how long will that be?" she asked.

The lawyer shook his head. "That will be up to the child-welfare department and how quickly they'll be able to find a home for her. At any rate, someone will be contacting you soon. So don't worry."

Nodding that she understood, she thanked him for taking time on New Year's Day to help her.

It wasn't until they'd said goodbye and gotten back into the car that Kathleen turned to Ross and said, "I don't want Stormy to go to some couple who already have a houseful of children! I want her to get the care and attention she needs."

"You should have made that clear to Mr. Montgomery," he said, as he reached to start the car.

Kathleen shrugged, a worried frown on her face. "I know. But I don't think he understands how I feel. And I know that you do."

"I do?"

She gave him a sidelong glance while arranging the blanket around the baby's face. "Yes, you do. You know that I love her and that I want her to be in a loving home. And you feel the very same way."

"Yes, I do," he said, his expression somber.

He steered the car out of the parking lot and onto the street. As he did, he noticed Kathleen was pressing her cheek against the baby's, and there were tears glistening in her eyes. The sight tore at his heart.

"Oh, Ross, when we were being questioned by those policemen and they kept talking about the real mother, I just wanted to scream at them that there was no other mother. That I was her mother! Is it crazy for me to feel this way?"

Her voice was quavering and he knew the past hour had shaken her more than she was letting on. "No, it isn't crazy. But..." He glanced at her, then wished he hadn't, because her tearful green eyes were looking at him, begging him for some kind of reassurance. He drew in a long breath, then let it out slowly. "Look, Kathleen, I think you're going to be hurt if you let your emotions get involved with this child. Pretty soon you're going to be telling me that you want to keep her for your own."

That idea had crossed Kathleen's mind more than once last night. She'd wanted a child for such a long time. Now it seemed as though God had intentionally placed one in her lap. This child needed a home. And this might be Kathleen's one and only chance of having a baby.

"I don't suppose I told you this, but I've wanted a child for a long time." She smoothed her fingertips over the baby's dark hair. "Why shouldn't I want to keep this one?"

"I don't know, Kathleen. But I imagine the fact that you're single would make it extra hard for you to permanently adopt her. Besides, it might turn out that she has other relatives around here who might want her."

Horrified, Kathleen tightened her hold on the baby. "Oh, Ross, you don't think they'd let them have her, do you?"

"Kathleen, I'm only wanting you to look at all possibilities. I don't want you to be disappointed."

Kathleen fished a tissue out of her purse and carefully dried her eyes. "I know, Ross. And I'm sorry for becoming emotional. I guess these past twenty-four hours have been more of a strain on me than I thought."

"Look, why don't you forget about all this for right now. You have custody for the time being. So let's take her to a doctor for a checkup and then we'll see about buying her a few things," he suggested.

"You're right. Today is the beginning of a brand new year. Let's enjoy what's left of it."

"Good. I might even take you out to eat later. To repay you for the breakfast you cooked for me," he added.

As she looked at him, her spirits began to lift and a smile curved her lips. "You've got a deal."

Chapter Eight

Stormy weighed six and a half pounds and the doctor pronounced her healthy and fit. He clamped off her umbilical cord, and gave Kathleen the name of a formula to start her on, plus several small booklets of information he felt would be helpful to her. Kathleen and Ross left the twenty-four-hour medical clinic feeling happy and relieved about the baby's physical condition.

They found a discount store that was open in spite of the day being a holiday, and the two of them quickly began to fill a shopping cart with baby formula, diapers, bottles and a baby carrier.

When they came to the clothes, and Kathleen started tossing in all sorts of garments, Ross didn't say a word to discourage her. He'd already seen her tears once today. And if buying the baby clothes made her happy, he wasn't going to be the one to spoil it for her.

They chose to eat at a nearby restaurant that specialized in home-cooked meals. Since it was New Year's Day, black-eyed peas, hog jowls and corn bread were offered with all the main courses.

"We have to eat black-eyed peas," Kathleen insisted, "so our year will be filled with good luck. Don't you believe that?"

While the waitress stood waiting for them to make up their minds, Ross gave Kathleen an indulgent smile. "If you believe it, Kathleen, then I'll eat them."

He handed the menu back to the waitress. "I'll take mine with fried catfish."

Kathleen decided on the same thing, then asked the waitress if she could prepare a bottle for Stormy. The woman kindly obliged, and while they waited for their meal, Kathleen fed the baby.

As she sat in the booth across from Ross and held the baby in her arms, she wondered if this was how it felt to have a real family, the family she'd always wanted. The baby wasn't hers. Neither was Ross, but just for tonight she wanted to pretend that she was a woman loved by this dark handsome man across from her. And in return for that love, she'd given him a beautiful daughter.

"You know, there really was an angel on your shoulder last night," Kathleen told him. "Because you came home and found the baby before the cold temperature had a chance to harm her."

Ross looked at his shoulder, then grinned at Kathleen. "An angel, huh? Well, I only hope she didn't hear all that cursing I did when I was trying to make it up the hill to your house."

"I'm sure in this case you've already been forgiven."

Since Stormy had now finished the bottle, Kathleen put her back in her new carrier. Even though she weighed next to nothing, Kathleen's arms were beginning to grow tired, and she knew it was better for the baby's neck and back to be well supported.

Their meal arrived just as she'd gotten the baby settled. While the two of them ate, Kathleen encouraged Ross to tell her about himself. "I feel as if you know all about me and my family," she told him. "So tell me something about you. Did you grow up in San Antonio?"

He nodded. "Just outside of the city. Have you ever been there?"

Kathleen shook her head. "No. I've been to east Texas. That's where my mother and father are going to retire this coming spring."

"Oh, well," he said, slicing into the filleted catfish, "then you should go down there sometime. It's beautiful. Everyone should go down the Riverwalk and see the Alamo."

Her eyes glided over his face, then down to his broad shoulders. He was wearing a beige shirt with tiny black stripes running through it. On any other man it would have been plain, she thought, but on Ross it was downright sexy. She found that her eyes kept returning to the dark column of his throat and wondered if he was that same tanned color all over.

Good Lord, she hadn't thought about a man like this since—well, not since she'd first fallen for Greg. And look where that had gotten her, she quickly reminded herself.

"Maybe I will," she told him. "Sometime."

Ross wanted to tell her that he'd take her to Texas, but stopped himself short. He'd already let himself get more involved with this woman than he'd intended to. He wasn't about to make promises for the future, no matter how much he would enjoy taking Kathleen down the romantic Riverwalk in San Antonio.

"So what really made you move up here?" she asked him. "Other than the chance to take over your friend's coaching position."

Ross shrugged. "Since I graduated late last fall, it was hard to find a teaching position. So when this one presented itself, I decided it was just what I was looking for."

"And what were you looking for?"

His gray eyes met hers across the table, and even though she'd been with him all day, she felt just as jolted by them now as she had this morning over breakfast.

"A school where academics are as important as sports. A school that took not only my baseball, but also my teaching ability seriously. Sports are a great part of learning, but knowledge is vital for success."

"And you should know. I'd say you've come full circle." He was a man who was obviously passionate about his work, Kathleen thought, and one who stood by his convictions. Her father and brothers were like that, too. Unlike Greg, who'd been easily swayed to change his beliefs, especially when he thought money was going to change hands.

"A lot of people think I'm crazy for being a teacher instead of picking a career that would have earned a lot bigger salary."

Kathleen shook her head. "Money isn't everything. My late husband made plenty of money, more money than I was certainly ever used to having. But he wasn't happy. At least not with me."

Her words shocked him. He hadn't expected her to tell him something so private. And now that she had, all he could think about was how happy it made him just to look at her, to be with her.

"I—I'm sorry," she said in an embarrassed whisper. She dropped her gaze to her plate. "I shouldn't have said that to you. I don't even know why I did."

Ross reached across the table and took her hand in his. "Kathleen, look at me."

She did and her heart surged with a feeling so warm, so achingly sweet that tears burned the back of her eyes.

"You can say anything you want to me. No matter what it is." His mouth curved into an encouraging smile. "We're friends now. Aren't we?"

Kathleen had never realized how special that one word was until now. "Yes, we are. And I'm glad."

It was dark by the time they left the restaurant. On the way back up the mountain Ross decided he had to stay in his own home that night. He knew he could no longer trust himself or his feelings where Kathleen was concerned. Alone with her, he'd be more than tempted to make love to her, and right now that was the last thing either of them needed.

When they reached Kathleen's house and he told her he was going home, she looked at him in surprise. "Oh, Ross, are you sure? I was planning on you staying here with me and Stormy tonight."

Ross felt cut to pieces by the disappointment on her face, but held fast to his decision. "I know you were. But now that Stormy has been checked by the doctor and you have everything you need, you'll be fine."

Kathleen had never been a weak, clinging vine and she certainly didn't want Ross to think her one now. "Of course I'll be fine. Why, there's thousands of single mothers out there. I can do it. And anyway, it was my choice to keep the baby. She's my responsibility, not yours."

Ross should have been relieved by her independent attitude. But he wasn't. He felt like a heel. And more than that, he felt left out, separated from the instant family he'd been a part of this past night and day.

But that was the way it had always been for Ross. His mother had shoved him off on his father; then, when his father had remarried and started having children, he'd shoved him back to Ross's mother. Then *she'd* remarried, and her new life and new children hadn't included him, either. By the time he'd graduated from high school he'd left home, vowing that he would never again stay where he wasn't wanted or needed.

"Yeah, well, if you need me, you know where I am. Goodbye, Kathleen."

"Goodbye," she told him, then watched with a puzzled frown as he hurried out the door. In the last few minutes he'd suddenly changed from a warm, caring friend to a distant stranger. What had she done or said? Or was he simply telling her he'd done his part—he'd saved the baby's life—and his involvement was over?

The idea filled her with loneliness. And even though she had the baby to care for she couldn't shake the sad feeling, or Ross Douglas, from her mind.

"Kathleen, are you sure about this?" Ella Gallagher asked her daughter. "Adoption is a big responsibility for a couple to consider. And you're single. You wouldn't have a father around to help raise the child. Believe me, honey, this is something you need to think about.''

Kathleen switched the telephone receiver to her other ear, then said, "I have thought about it, Mother. I've thought about it ever since I first held her in my arms. Oh, Mom, she's just so precious and beautiful.''

Ella let out a knowing sigh. "Yes, I know, Kathleen, all babies are precious and beautiful. Then they grow up into precocious teenagers. Raising a baby to adulthood is not a snap, believe me.''

Kathleen frowned as she tried to butter her breakfast toast with the phone jammed between her shoulder and her ear. "So you're trying to discourage me. You think I'd be making a mistake. Mother, you know how much I've wanted a child!''

"I do know, Kathleen. So does your father. And we want you to have a child just as much as you do. It's only that we wanted you to have it with a husband.''

"Well, I wanted it that way, too. But it just didn't happen." She paused and took a deep breath. "Look, Mom, I might as well tell you that I called Parker Montgomery first thing this morning and told him my decision to try to adopt Stormy.''

"And what did he say?''

"Basically, that the circumstances of her real parents will have to be dealt with. If the authorities can find them. And also that my being single won't help matters. But he also said that it doesn't rule out my chances, either.''

Ella was silent for so long that Kathleen wondered if she'd fallen over in a faint. "Mother! Are you still there?"

"Yes, yes, I'm still here. I was just thinking."

"Thinking what?" she asked urgently. If there was one thing Kathleen needed now it was the support of her family, and she was praying they'd give it to her.

"That if this is what you really want, then you know your father and I will help you all we can."

Tears stung Kathleen's eyes. "I love you."

"If you do, then you'll come over tonight for supper and bring the baby. We're all dying to see her. And bring that young man who found her, too. We'd like to meet him."

"How do you know he's young? I didn't tell you that."

Ella laughed. "I knew he had to be young, because an old man certainly couldn't have carried a baby up that mountain in a snowstorm. Except maybe your daddy," she bragged, then laughed impishly.

Always amazed at her mother's deductions, Kathleen smiled and rolled her eyes. "You're right, he's young and he's handsome. And I'll try to get him and the baby there before you all sit down to eat."

"We'll be looking for you," Ella said, then after a quick goodbye, hung up the telephone.

By three o'clock that afternoon, Kathleen didn't know what to do about inviting Ross to dinner at the farmhouse. She'd been sure that he'd be back to check on her and the baby today, but so far she'd seen nothing of him. Since it was Saturday, she knew he wouldn't be at school teaching. And since he was new in the area, she really doubted he was visiting friends.

Well, if he didn't show up soon, she thought, she'd get in the car and drive to his house. He might not want to see her, but she wanted to see him. And since Kathleen had never been bashful, she wouldn't mind telling him that, or inviting him to have dinner with her and her family.

Ross stood by the picture window in his front room and absently lifted the coffee cup to his lips as he stared at the wooded hillside that led up to Kathleen's house. All day long he'd kept himself busy, unpacking boxes and putting the last of his things away. And all the while he'd worked, he'd thought about Kathleen and the baby. He missed them both, and the more he told himself he didn't need to see them, the more he wanted to see them.

Damn it, Ross, you're twenty-nine years old, he silently argued with himself. You've gone this long without letting a woman get under your skin. Just because Kathleen looks like a black-haired goddess and tastes like a piece of heaven doesn't mean you need her in your life.

But he did need her. He felt as empty as hell without her around him. So why was he fighting it? Why didn't he drive up the mountain and see her?

Because he had this crazy feeling that once he saw her again, he wouldn't be able to stop himself from falling in love with her. If he hadn't already.

Kathleen had just changed into a long, plaid wool skirt of deep browns and russets, a white blouse and a pair of fawn-colored dress boots when she heard the doorbell ring. Tossing her hairbrush aside, she hurried to answer it.

The moment she opened the door and saw Ross standing there with a wry grin on his face, her heart leaped with joy.

"Ross! I've been looking for you all day. I was about to think you'd forgotten all about me and Stormy."

As if he could, Ross thought, as she took him by the arm and led him into the house.

"No. I hadn't forgotten. I've been working—trying to get my things unpacked and put away." He wasn't going to admit he'd only now decided to come see her. And maybe that decision had been a mistake, he thought. But he didn't think so. Now that he was here, seeing the smile on her face, he felt good inside. He felt some unexplainable joy that he'd never felt in his life.

"How's the baby? Did she keep you awake last night?"

Kathleen led him over to the couch where Stormy lay sleeping. "She's fine. And no, she only woke up once during the night."

Kathleen wasn't going to admit to Ross that *he* was the reason she'd lost sleep last night, not the baby. She'd lived alone for more than a year now, but she couldn't remember a time when the house had seemed so quiet and empty. Even the baby's presence couldn't make up for Ross not being with her. But she couldn't tell him that. It would make it sound like she was falling in love with him. And she wasn't, was she?

Ross took a seat beside the baby and found he couldn't stop himself from touching her fine baby hair and the soft little curve of her cheek. Kathleen had put a dress on her. It was white, with little red bows and hearts embroidered across the front. She looked like a little dark-haired cherub.

"She looks all dressed up now. Nothing like the pathetic little mite I found in that cardboard box."

Kathleen smiled down at both of them. Now that Ross was with them, she felt complete. "I just changed her clothes a few minutes ago. I'm taking her over to meet my family. That is, *we're* taking her over. You're invited, too."

His head jerked up. "Me? Oh, no—no, I couldn't be invited. Your family doesn't even know me!"

Kathleen laughed at his shocked expression. "Of course they don't know you. That's why they want to meet you. You've become a hero, you know."

Ross shook his head in dismay. "Damn it, I'm not a hero. I'm not anything close to it."

"Well, when Stormy grows up, she's going to thank you," Kathleen told him.

He looked back at the baby. Would he mean anything to this tiny little girl when she grew to be a woman? Would she even be a part of his life? The questions made him realize what a loss it would be not to have children in his life. And even more, what a loss it would be not to have a part in this child's life.

"Are you sure your family really invited me? You're not just pushing me on them?"

Kathleen laughed. "You can't push anyone on the Gallaghers, believe me."

"Well, I'm not exactly dressed for a family dinner."

Her gaze quickly took in his jeans and boots, and black-and-red letter jacket. "You're not naked under that jacket, are you?" she asked impishly.

With a crooked grin on his mouth, he pulled back one side of the jacket to show her he was wearing a plain black T-shirt.

"You're perfect," she assured him with a wave of her hand. "So I'll get Stormy's carrier and diaper bag and we'll be off."

Ross had never been invited by a woman to meet her parents or family before, and he wasn't quite sure he wanted to go. But since Kathleen was with him and they were already halfway to the farm, he could hardly turn around and run for his life.

"My brother Sam is the quiet, serious one of us. Nick is the teasing prankster who's been pestering me ever since he was old enough to try," Kathleen told him as they turned into the lane leading up to the farmhouse.

"And your serious brother Sam always came along and stood up for you."

She laughed. "How did you know?"

Ross could hear the fondness in her voice as she spoke of her brothers, and he wondered what it would be like to hold such a place in her heart. She was a special woman. And the man she loved would have to be special. Not someone like him.

"Just a guess," he answered.

Kathleen glanced over at him, her eyes sliding appreciatively over his strong profile. "Oh, you probably have a brother or sister just like that, don't you?"

A faint frown passed over his features. "I don't have any brothers or sisters."

Clearly puzzled, she stared at him. "But you said you had two sets of half brothers and sisters."

He nodded, his expression stoic. "I do. Two brothers. Three sisters. But I don't consider them real brothers and sisters. They were just kids I grew up around, some of them for longer periods than others."

How terribly sad, Kathleen thought. She couldn't imagine her life without Nick or Sam, or the love and companionship they shared with each other. And it hurt her to think that Ross had never known that kind of love and closeness.

When Kathleen and Ross entered the house, they found the whole family in the den. Even Jake and Leo, Sam's two collies, were stretched out asleep on the fireplace hearth.

"Here they are," S.T. boomed when he spotted his daughter coming through the doorway.

S.T.'s announcement caused a stir of commotion, and Ross suddenly found himself, Kathleen and the baby surrounded. As his eyes quickly darted over the group, he registered three tall, strongly built men and three very attractive women.

"Okay," Kathleen said as everyone started to talk at once. "This is Ross Douglas." Smiling, she looked at Ross who was still close to her elbow. "Ross, this is my mother and father," she said proudly.

Ross nodded at the older, but still-handsome couple. "Nice to meet you, ma'am. Mr. Gallagher."

"Same here, Ross. And it's Ella and S.T. We don't go for that formal stuff around here," S.T. told him.

Kathleen continued to introduce the rest of the group to Ross. "And this stony-faced one in the flannel shirt is my brother Sam. And the beauty he's hanging onto is his new wife, Olivia."

"Hello, Sam, Olivia," Ross greeted them both.

Kathleen motioned her hand to the last two adults. "This handsome thing is my brother Nick, the rebel. And of course, that's his sweet fiancée, Allison. Oh, and over by Jake and Leo is little Ben, Allison's son."

Ross's gaze circled the whole group. "It's very nice to meet Kathleen's family. I only hope I'm not intruding."

"Nonsense, boy! We Gallaghers always like to see an extra face around here," S.T. told him.

"That's right, so let's see the baby," Nick told Kathleen. "You've got her hidden under all those blankets. Are you trying to suffocate her, sis?"

Kathleen rolled her eyes at her brother. "Not hardly. It's cold outside, or do you realize that, now that you're in love?"

Grinning wickedly, Nick looked at Allison. "Did you know it was cold outside?" he asked her, then looked back at his sister, his expression an exaggeration of innocence. "We didn't know, sis."

"Give me that baby! I'll not stand around and wait while you two bicker," Ella said. She took Stormy from Kathleen and carried her over to the couch.

Everyone followed, and as Ella peeled back the baby blankets, they crowded around for a look.

"Oh, my. Look at her, Sam," Olivia said in a hushed voice. "Isn't she precious?"

"And look at all that dark hair!" Allison exclaimed. "Benjamin was nearly bald when he was born."

"We can have that buzzed off in no time," Nick teased, making the women groan.

"She's not one of your soldiers, Nick," Kathleen scolded him, although her voice was filled with affection.

"I can't believe someone left her in a storm," Sam said, his voice full of disbelief and outrage.

"Neither can I," S.T. put in. "Whoever did it ought to be strung up by the heels and hung out to dry."

Ella, who had yet to say a word, looked up at her husband, her eyes glistening with tears. "S.T., she looks just like Kathleen did when she was born."

S.T. patted his wife's shoulder. "Now, honey, you know that can't be."

"S.T., don't argue with me," she said with a sniff. "I ought to know. I suffered through twelve hours of labor to get her born. I should know what she looked like when she finally did come out. And it was just like this. A mass of black hair. And those eyes—they'll turn green before she's a year old. I'll bet you anything they do."

S.T. chuckled fondly at his wife's prediction. "I can see you've already christened her a Gallagher."

"Well, she will be a Gallagher if Kathleen is able to adopt her."

Adopt her! Ross went rigid with shock. Was Kathleen going to try to adopt Stormy?

Chapter Nine

"I think this calls for a toast," S.T. said. "Sam, you and Nick go pour everybody a round of that wine your mama had left over from New Year's Eve."

Wine was passed around and glasses were raised to the new baby. Ross looked at Kathleen, to see her face was glowing with joy as she watched her family fuss over Stormy.

"Kathleen?"

When she turned to answer, he took her by the arm and led her across the room, away from the others.

"What is this about adopting Stormy? You didn't say anything to me about adopting her."

Kathleen suddenly felt incredibly guilty. She'd wanted to tell Ross of her decision. In fact, she'd wanted to tell him before she'd told anyone else. But a part of her had been afraid he'd try to dissuade her. "I know. I was going to, later."

Why did he suddenly feel so left out? Her family had obviously already learned of her decision to adopt the baby. But he hadn't. Hell, Ross, he scolded himself, she loves her family. You didn't expect her to treat you the same way, did you?

"So you have decided to adopt her?" he asked.

Wanting and needing to feel the reassurance of his touch, she reached for his hand and threaded her fingers through his. "I know that I'm single and that I might have trouble getting her. But I have to try, Ross. I've fallen in love with her. I can't just let her go."

And Ross had fallen in love with Kathleen. He didn't know when, or how it had happened. But it had. And as he looked at her now, surrounded by this big, loving family, he wondered where, if at all, he could possibly fit in.

Dinner was a big meal of plain, home-cooked food and boisterous conversation. Ross was told all sorts of stories that ranged from farming incidents, to childhood pranks, to Allison's account of how she'd accepted Nick's engagement ring only because she'd been afraid he'd throw it into the hog pen if she refused.

Ross enjoyed all the anecdotes, and even more, he enjoyed being with Kathleen's family. They were an open bunch who said what they thought, and whatever they were curious to know about him they asked outright, instead of digging at him with sly innuendos and subtle questions.

After supper the men took their coffee to the den, while Olivia and Allison insisted Kathleen go upstairs with them to look at a dress in a brides' magazine.

"But what about Stormy?" she protested, as the two women urged her up the stairs.

"Ella is already in there changing her diaper," Olivia assured her. "She'll be fine."

When they entered Kathleen's old bedroom and shut the door, she looked around the room. "Okay, where's the magazine? Is the dress short or long?"

Allison looked uncomfortable, while Olivia giggled. "There is no magazine. I mean, there is, but Allison is still trying to decide about a dress for herself, first. We wanted you up here for other reasons."

Kathleen looked at both women. "What other reasons?"

Allison smiled. "We've heard all about the baby. We sorta—well..."

"There's no 'sorta' about it. We want to know about Ross," Olivia finished for her.

Kathleen's brows arched upward. "You've already asked him everything. I'm surprised Sam didn't ask him for his Social Security number!"

Olivia and Allison burst out laughing, but Kathleen merely glared at the two of them. "What's so funny about it? I imagine Ross feels like he stepped under a microscope instead of into a farmhouse!"

"Oh, I'm sure he doesn't feel that way at all," Allison put in. "He seems to be enjoying himself. Especially when he looks at you, Kathleen."

Kathleen could suddenly see where the two women's thoughts were heading and she threw up her hands to quickly put a stop to it. "You're imagining that. Besides, I met the man less than three days ago!"

Allison looked at Olivia. "Remember when I was saying the very same thing about Nick?"

Olivia nodded smugly. "I remember it vividly. It was on my wedding day. And now you're happily engaged and soon to be married."

"Okay, okay," Kathleen conceded, as she sank down into a wooden rocking chair. "So I did badger you two about your love lives with my brothers. But this is different. Ross is...well, he is special. And I...really like him. A lot. But, well, it's not like what you two have with Sam and Nick. Ross isn't thinking that way toward me. Why, he so much as told me that he's purposely steered clear of love and marriage."

"Hmm. That's just what Nick told me," Allison said as she exchanged a knowing little smile with Olivia.

"So are you thinking that way toward him?" Olivia asked.

Kathleen's mouth formed a surprised O. Was she thinking about Ross in those terms? "Olivia, you know what I went through with Greg! Our marriage was horrible. He cheated on me and I...well, I've just gotten my life back together again. Why would I want to become involved with a man?"

"Some of us can't seem to help it," Allison said softly, then glanced once again at Olivia.

"Well, from what you've told me, I can't see where Ross is anything like Greg." Olivia walked over and took a seat on the side of the bed, then looked back at Kathleen. "In fact, I think the whole family likes him."

"I'm glad," Kathleen told her. "As I said, I like him, too."

"You know," Allison put in, "you did catch Olivia's wedding bouquet. I think that really did mean something."

Kathleen's laughter was full of disbelief. "What makes you think so?"

"Well, a tall, dark man has come into your life. Plus a baby. I can't think of a better sign."

"You know," Olivia added impishly, "Ross reminds me of a black-haired James Dean. He has that roguish sort of charm, I think. And when he smiles, that little dimple next to his mouth... well, he's anything but ugly, Kathleen."

"Shame on you! I'm going to tell Sam you have roving eyes already!"

Olivia laughed like a woman who was sure of her man and her marriage. "Sam knows I love only him. And that's the way it will always be."

Kathleen looked at her sisters-in-law and felt a pang of envy. These two women had men who loved and adored them. And more than likely they would soon have children. Kathleen might never have either.

"Kathleen, why don't you and Ross come back tomorrow and have Sunday dinner with us," Ella said later that night as Kathleen and Ross were preparing to leave. "I haven't gotten to hold this baby nearly enough."

"Good idea," Nick spoke up. "Come on back, Ross. Sam has this idea that we *have* to cut firewood tomorrow. He'll put you to work."

Later, when Ross pulled his pickup to a stop in front of her house, Kathleen said, "You don't want to go to the farm tomorrow. I can tell."

"Why do you say that?"

Kathleen looked at him. He'd been so quiet and withdrawn on the way home. Kathleen could only imagine that he was regretting spending the evening with her and her family. "I don't know. Just a feeling."

He let out a tense breath. All the way home, Ross had felt her beside him. He wanted more than anything to touch her, to kiss her again, and he wondered what her reaction would be if he did.

"Your family was crazy about Stormy," he said, reaching to switch off the motor.

Kathleen smiled at the baby who was strapped in her safety seat. "Yes, they were." She glanced back at him. "They liked you, too."

He made a sound of disbelief. "Oh, yeah? How could you tell?"

"I just could. You know what Olivia said about you?"

He gave her a wary look from the corner of his eye. "No. What?"

"She said you reminded her of a black-haired James Dean."

Ross threw back his head and laughed. "I guess that's a compliment."

"She meant it as such," Kathleen said as she reached to unstrap the baby carrier.

"Here, let me carry Stormy into the house for you," Ross offered. "I don't want either of you to get hurt on the ice."

Kathleen handed him the baby, then quickly gathered her purse and diaper bag from the floorboard of the pickup. Once they made it into the house, Kathleen had him carry the baby on to her bedroom.

"Since the bed is king-size, I let her sleep with me," Kathleen told him as they walked down the hall. "That way I can hear her if she cries."

A dim shaft of light from the hall slanted across the large room, showing Ross the way to the bed. Kathleen followed closely behind him and switched on a small table lamp as he gently placed the baby on the bed.

Since Stormy was already wearing footed pajamas, Kathleen carefully covered her with blankets, then placed pillows on either side of her. "I know she won't be able to roll for a long time yet, but it gives me a sense of security to have them there just in case," she told Ross.

Straightening up from her task, she looked at him and smiled. "Maybe I should look into getting a baby bed."

"Kathleen . . ."

She could see all sorts of doubts crossing his face and knew what he was going to say. "I know, Ross. You're going to tell me I shouldn't get my hopes up."

She was only a step away. Ross closed the distance and put his hand on her shoulder. "You'll be hurt if you have to give her up. And I don't want to see that happen to you."

Kathleen's eyes searched his face, and as she did, her heart began to hammer in her breast. The look in his gray eyes wasn't just one of concern, it was also a look of desire.

"Then I hope you'll keep your fingers crossed for me," she said, unaware that her voice had dropped to little more than a whisper.

In that moment, as Ross gazed down at her, he realized he'd do anything to make this woman happy. "I will."

His hand was warm upon Kathleen's shoulder and the subtle scent of his masculine cologne teased her nostrils. Except for the baby, they were completely alone. And her whole body began to quiver with anticipation.

"About going back to the farm with you tomorrow," he murmured, "I'd like to. If you want me to."

His words pleased her far more than she wanted to admit, and before she realized what she was doing, she rose up on tiptoe and kissed his cheek. "I'm glad. I do want you to go."

The moment her lips touched his face, Ross was lost. His hands meshed in her thick hair and held her cheek close against his.

"Oh, Kathleen, you are the most beautiful woman I've ever seen," he whispered fervently. His fingers moved to her face, where he touched her eyes, her nose, her cheeks and finally her lips. "Do you know how much I want to kiss you? Hold you in my arms?"

His words and the urgency of his fingertips on her face echoed Kathleen's own feelings, and she was helpless to resist him or the desire coursing through her body. His name rose up in her throat, but before it could pass her lips, he'd taken her into his arms and covered her mouth with his.

Kathleen had forgotten nothing about the kiss they'd shared on New Year's Eve, and as she surrendered her lips to his, she found she didn't have to go looking for the same passion she'd felt that night. It was already there, burning like a flame between them.

Ross had never been so lost in his life. He forgot where he was, or the long minutes slowing ticking by. He forgot everything as his senses blurred and became consumed by the woman in his arms. She smelled like red roses in the hot sun, and her lips were soft, velvety and achingly sweet. The feel of her ripe curves pressing into him made him shake with the need to make love to her.

"Kathleen!"

Her head spun dizzily as he breathed her name and scattered kisses across her cheek. By the time his teeth sank gently into her earlobe, she was clinging desperately to his waist.

"Oh, Ross, this is madness! I don't think—"

"No. Don't think," he said thickly, "just let me kiss you."

His lips were on her face, pressing kisses along the curve of her jaw. With a tormented groan, Kathleen's head fell limply back, allowing him access to the smooth column of her throat.

His lips quickly followed the V of her blouse until he reached the button above her heart. Then his fingers quickly went to work, until finally the fabric fell away to expose her creamy breasts encased in white lace. A low, guttural sound was torn from Ross's throat as he bent his head even lower.

Katherine wanted him to make love to her. She'd never wanted anything so badly in her life. So why shouldn't she give in to this magic he was working on her? she asked herself. Why shouldn't she let his body appease this burning ache within her?

The answer to that question left her groaning inside. She wanted this to be lovemaking, not just a sexual encounter. And it *would* be making love on her part. She realized that now. She loved this dark-haired man with his crooked smile and cool gray eyes. And she wanted him to love her back. Not just with his body, but with his heart.

"Ross, I can't. I—this is too soon," she whispered brokenly.

Her fingers threaded into the dark waves of his hair and urged his head up to hers.

"My God, Kathleen! Don't ask me to stop now! Do you know how much I want you?"

Yes, she knew it. Because she wanted him just as badly. "I know. But I'm... just not ready for this."

Drawing in a ragged breath, he turned away from her. "No, I guess you're not," he said huskily.

"Please don't be angry with me," she whispered.

"Don't apologize, Kathleen," he said in a tormented voice.

Sensing she'd hurt him more than angered him, Kathleen placed a tentative hand against his back. "Whatever you might think of me, Ross, I don't go around tempting men to make love to me."

He knew that. In fact, he doubted she'd ever made love to a man outside the sanctity of marriage. "Well, whatever you might think, I don't go around trying to make love to every woman who gets within a foot of *me*."

She sighed wistfully. "I don't imagine you do."

He turned back to her. "I guess after this...well, if you want to cancel tomorrow, I'll understand."

Wide-eyed, she stared at him. "Cancel? No. I don't want to cancel anything!" Reaching for his hands, she threaded her fingers through his. "Ross, I still want us to be friends! I mean, we can forget about this and still be together, can't we?"

She expected them to be together, like friends? After what they'd just shared? She must think he was superhuman! How could he resist her? How could he look at her and not remember what it felt like to hold her, kiss her?

"I don't know, Kathleen. I—"

Hearing the hesitation in his voice, she said, "Look, Ross, you told me you wanted no part of marriage. And I can certainly understand that. That's why I think... well, I guess I'm old-fashioned, because I realize I couldn't make love to a man unless he was committed to me. And I'd never ask that of you. Anyway, I've vowed a thousand times I'd never marry again."

Ross had said all that, and he respected everything she was telling him. But the truth was, he no longer felt that way. He wanted to tell Kathleen that he was committed to her. And that if she wanted it, his heart was hers.

But Ross had been shut out so many times before that he was afraid to expose his true feelings. And from what she was saying to him now, it was all for the best that she didn't know how he really felt. She wanted no part of him, or any man.

"I, uh, I gotta get out of here. I'll see you tomorrow," he muttered.

Feeling wounded but not really understanding why, Kathleen watched him leave the room. Moments later, she heard a door slam and knew he'd left the house. Maybe forever, she thought sickly.

"Damn it! Damn it all," she whispered fiercely. Why had this happened? Why couldn't they have kept their hands off of each other? she asked herself, tears forming in her eyes. Now everything had changed. Everything! And she was terrified of what this change might do to her already scarred heart.

The next morning, while Kathleen was getting ready to go to the farm for Sunday dinner, she wondered how she would be able to face Ross and act as though everything was normal.

Everything was far from normal, she thought; in fact, she was a wreck and she looked it. She'd slept little, if any. Not because Stormy had awakened twice in the night. No, it had been a little more complicated than that. She hadn't been able to get Ross out of her mind. Every time she'd closed her eyes, his image had been right there in front of her, tempting her, troubling her with all sorts of thoughts.

She didn't know how she'd let herself fall in love with him. Since her disastrous marriage to Greg, she'd believed she would never be capable of loving again. But on New Year's Eve, Ross had walked into her house and into her heart.

Sometimes we can't help ourselves. Allison's words about falling in love were coming home to Kathleen. Because now she understood that loving a person wasn't something you could make happen, or something that you could prevent. Good or bad, it just happened.

When Ross arrived a few minutes later, Kathleen felt her heart stirring in spite of herself. He had come back.

"Good morning," she said as she shut the door behind him.

"Good morning," he said, his gray eyes slipping over her face. She looked tired this morning, and he wondered if the baby had kept her awake. "How did it go with the baby last night?"

Smiling briefly, she motioned for him to take a seat. "It went fine," she said, which was true enough. It just hadn't been fine without him. She'd missed him. Every waking minute she spent without him, she missed him. It was crazy. She knew having him near was a dreadful temptation, but it was equally dreadful for her when he was gone.

Ignoring the couch, Ross went to stand by the fireplace. "She didn't wake up?" he asked.

"Only twice."

He should have been here to help her, Ross thought. A woman shouldn't have to care for a baby without the help of a man. Even though Stormy hadn't been born to them, he felt as though Kathleen was her mother and he was her father. And parents needed to live under the same roof together. They needed to share the same dinner table, the same bed. Ross knew that better than anyone.

"I woke up last night thinking I heard her cry," he admitted. "I couldn't go back to sleep."

Something akin to pain wound around Kathleen's heart. She knew he'd grown close to the baby. It was probably hard on him to be away from her, not to be able to hold her or see for himself that she was all right. As this thought passed through Kathleen's head, it dawned on her that she and Ross were almost like a divorced couple with a baby in between. It was no wonder that Ross didn't want to have a family, she thought. He knew firsthand what kind of pain went along with torn marriages.

"You shouldn't have worried," she said huskily. "You knew I'd be here to take care of her."

He looked at her, taking in her long black hair, her ruby red lips, her tall, lush figure beneath the shirtdress she was wearing. She was achingly beautiful and Ross knew it was a good thing they were going to be around her family today. Otherwise, all he could think about was going over to her and unbuttoning the long row of black buttons on her dress, kissing her mouth and carrying her to bed.

Dragging in a heavy breath, he looked away from her. "Yes, I knew you were here to take care of her," he said quietly, "but I worried just the same."

Kathleen crossed the room to him and instinctively put her hand on his arm. "I don't want you to worry about Stormy, Ross. You can come check on her anytime. Even if it is the middle of the night."

His gaze went from where Kathleen was touching him up to her face. "I don't think that would be a good idea, Kathleen."

Stabbed by his words, she quickly dropped her hand and tucked it behind her back, as though keeping it hidden would help her to quit touching him.

"Maybe you're right," she murmured, unaware of how sad she sounded. She didn't know why she felt so hurt and rejected. She'd made it clear to him last night that she didn't want anything physical between them. What was she going to do? She felt torn up inside.

After several tense moments passed and Ross didn't say anything, Kathleen let out a long breath and said, "So, if you're ready, maybe we'd better be going. Mother usually fries chicken on Sunday. We don't want to be late."

After dinner, S.T. turned on a football game and the women took the baby upstairs. Nick and Sam invited Ross to help them cut firewood.

"We don't usually make our guests work," Nick told him, as the three men drove across the east pasture in Sam's pickup, "but you've been promoted from guest to friend of the family now. So that means you *have* to work."

"Just keep a close eye on Nick," Sam warned Ross, "or he'll be sitting on the tailgate, while you and I do all the work."

Ross smiled, enjoying the companionship of Kathleen's brothers. "Maybe I'd better warn y'all that I haven't done much woodcutting. Where I come from, we didn't need much heat."

Nick laughed and slapped him on the shoulder. "Boy, have you come to the right place to learn about using a chain saw. Sam thinks a man hasn't lived until he's had a chain saw in his hands."

"It's a damn sight safer than that M16 you tote around," Sam said dryly. "And more useful, too."

"Is that so? Well, who had to go get ten stitches in his leg last winter? It wasn't me and my M16," Nick said, sharing a wink with Ross.

An hour later, all three men were sweating in spite of the cold weather. They had the pickup half-loaded with cut hardwood and had decided to take a little breather. Sam had brought a thermos of coffee and he passed cups to Nick and Ross, who were sharing a seat on the open tailgate.

"You know, Ross," he said, "Nick and I are both glad to see you with Kathleen. She's had a hell of a time of it this past year."

Ross looked down at the brown liquid in his cup. "She told me about her husband being killed. I guess it's been hard for her to get over."

Nick shook his head. "Hard? I was honestly beginning to think she was going to grieve forever."

Sam frowned. "I don't really think she was griev-ing. I think Greg left her downright sick."

Nick nodded. "You're right about that. He made her life miserable." His eyes narrowed with recollec-tion. "You know, the first time I ever laid eyes on the man, I knew I didn't like him. He was a self-absorbed son-of-a—" He glanced at Ross. "Well, you get the picture, don't you?"

Ross nodded. He got the picture all too well, and it made him sick to think of Kathleen being hurt by a man, or hurt by anything, for that matter.

"Anyway," Sam said, "we're glad she's taken to you. We didn't think she'd ever look at another man. You're just what she needs."

Kathleen's brothers thought she was looking at him like that? They thought Kathleen needed him? He'd never been needed in his life. "You two have it all wrong if you think Kathleen is taken with me. It's not like that at all."

Nick and Sam exchanged knowing glances. "Oh," Nick said, "I guess we were wrong. We just thought from the way she looked at you that you and she were . . . well, getting close."

Maybe they had gotten close, but Kathleen was see-ing to it that they didn't get any closer. "Kathleen is all caught up in the baby. She's not thinking about me."

Sam exchanged another look with his brother. "Yeah," he said to Ross, "Kathleen has wanted a baby for a long time. But just between the three of us, I don't think she has a prayer in hell of adopting Stormy."

"I agree," Nick said grimly. "I can't see a judge handing that baby over to Kathleen when there are plenty of two-parent families out there just begging to adopt a child.''

Ross looked from Nick to Sam, then back to Nick. ''It will kill her if she doesn't get to keep that baby,'' he said.

''We know. That's why we're glad she has you,'' Sam said. ''She's going to need you to help her get over the disappointment.''

Chapter Ten

That's why we're glad she has you. Sam's words haunted Ross through the remainder of the day. And that night, on the drive home from the Gallaghers', he came to a decision.

"Do you mind if I come in, Kathleen?" he asked when he pulled the truck to a stop in Kathleen's driveway. "There's something I want to talk to you about."

For the bigger part of the day, Ross had kept his distance from Kathleen, so his request surprised her, to say the least. "What is it?" she asked him after they'd gathered Stormy and her things and gone into the house.

He motioned toward the baby. "Let's get her into bed first," he said.

"All right," she agreed, wondering at his serious tone. What was it? Was he going to tell her that he thought it would be better if he didn't see her or the baby anymore? The mere thought shook her.

Once Kathleen had Stormy settled in bed, she kicked off her shoes and went to the kitchen to make a fresh pot of coffee. Ross followed, wondering how he was going to manage talking to her for more than five minutes without putting his hands on her.

"I hope my family hasn't hurt you in some way. Mother and Nick can be so direct at times. I hope neither of them said anything that angered you."

He waved away her suggestion and leaned against the counter a step or two from her. "It's nothing like that. Your family is wonderful. They've gone out of their way to be nice to me," Ross said. Then, deciding it would be better if he put some distance between them, he took a seat at the table in the middle of the room. "But your family is not what's on my mind. I've been doing a lot of thinking these past two days...."

Kathleen switched on the coffee machine, then turned and rested against the counter. "About what?" she asked, hoping she didn't sound as nervous as she felt.

"About me and you, and Stormy."

Kathleen's heart began to thud so hard she felt lightheaded. "What about us?"

Unable to keep his distance, Ross got up from the table and came to stand in front of her. There was a strange lump in his throat as he looked at her. "I think you and I should get married."

Kathleen was so stunned her knees threatened to buckle beneath her. "Married! What are you saying, Ross?"

He wanted to sound casual and unaffected, but he knew he couldn't keep the emotions he was feeling out of his voice. He'd never loved a woman before. He'd never been brave enough to let himself. But his heart was on the line now and he'd never been more afraid.

"I'm saying that if you really want to have a chance of adopting Stormy, we need to get married. Of course, it would be in name only, but the courts wouldn't have to know that."

Dazed, Kathleen stared at him. "You mean you'd do that for me? For her?"

He nodded, and Kathleen realized if she hadn't been leaning against the counter, she would have fallen. Ross was willing to marry her for her and the baby's sake. It was one of the most unselfish gestures Kathleen had ever heard of. But on the other hand, she realized a part of her was deeply wounded because he wasn't proposing to her out of real love.

"I can't imagine—" She broke off as her eyes searched his. "Are you really serious?"

His hands curved around her shoulders. "I'm very serious. I want you to have Stormy." He wanted that almost as much as he wanted her to be his wife. And he'd do anything to make both of those things happen.

Kathleen turned away from him. She knew she had to. Otherwise, she might become so mesmerized by his touch, she'd be tempted to say yes.

"I'm sorry, Ross. I couldn't marry you under those circumstances. I couldn't marry you under *any* circumstances."

Without looking at him, she turned and left the room. Ross followed her down the hallway and out to the living room. "Why can't you?" he asked. "What could it possibly hurt? You could get the baby you've always wanted. And I'd know she was where she belonged. Then later on—if you wanted—we could get a divorce.''

A divorce! How many times had Greg flung that word at her? she wondered hysterically. She hadn't been able to give him the child he wanted. She hadn't been able to make him happy. He'd wanted a divorce so he could find a woman who could do both of those things.

Now the thought of Ross using that same word with her made Kathleen feel like she'd been cut with a dirty knife. ''I don't want to be married! Don't you understand that, Ross?''

She walked rigidly to the windows overlooking the front lawn. Ross followed and stood just behind her. ''I understand that you had a bad marriage. Your brothers told me what a bastard Greg was. But that has nothing to do with you and me. You wouldn't be marrying me for love.''

Kathleen felt like a lance had been thrust through her heart. She *would* be marrying Ross for love. That's why she couldn't marry him. She'd be setting herself up for all kinds of hurt. She wanted Stormy desperately, but she couldn't risk that kind of involvement just to help her chances for adoption.

She let out a brittle laugh. ''I had something worse than a bad marriage, Ross. And the crazy thing about it, I didn't even realize how bad it was until Greg was killed. I guess for the three years we were married I closed my eyes. I wanted to believe that everything was all right. But when he died . . . I had to finally face facts.''

Before he could say anything, Kathleen whirled around to face him. "What did my brothers really tell you? Did they tell you that when my husband went down in that plane, his mistress was with him?"

Ross was sickened by the dark image Kathleen was painting for him. "You mean . . . she died with him?"

Her features stiff, Kathleen gave one nod. "Yes. Poor thing. Sometimes I think fate dealt her a kinder hand by taking her life instead of letting her live and continue to love Greg Hayes. He would have only wound up hurting her, too."

"Oh, Kathleen, what a thing to live with! Did you know about her before the accident?"

She made a little sound of self-mockery. "I had my suspicions, but I turned a blind eye to them. I kept thinking . . ."

Unable to go on, Kathleen looked away from him. She couldn't tell Ross that she'd continued on with Greg, hoping and believing that if she could become pregnant and give him a child, their marriage would turn around and become the family she'd always wanted. She couldn't bear for this man to know that she was infertile, something less than a woman.

"It doesn't matter what I thought. I can't marry you, Ross. I'll never marry anyone!"

Ross shook his head with frustration. "But this would be different, Kathleen. This wouldn't be a real marriage where hearts and emotions are involved. It would just be a legal convenience, that's all."

A legal convenience! How could he talk about something as sacred as marriage in such a way? She'd thought he was different from other men. She'd thought he had moral dignity, but apparently he viewed marriage the same way Greg had. It was just a convenience for whatever served their purposes.

"How could you say that to me?" she whispered fiercely. Hot tears spurted from her eyes. "You're just like Greg was. Marriage means nothing to you! It's only a way to get what you want at the time you're wanting it. And if it doesn't work out—well," she said with a bitter laugh, "what the hell, there's always divorce. It doesn't matter that marriage is supposed to be holy, that it's supposed to last for life!"

With a little sob she turned away from him and covered her face with her hands. "I don't want to talk about this anymore, Ross."

Ross had never felt so bewildered as when he watched her slumped shoulders shake with silent sobs. He hadn't expected her to react this way. Before he'd asked her to marry him, he'd tried to steel himself against a rejection, because he'd expected one. But Ross hadn't expected such an emotional one, and he couldn't understand it. He wasn't asking her to love him, though he knew how much he wanted her love. He was trying to help her. Couldn't she see that?

He ventured closer and touched her arm. "I didn't ask you to marry me as a way to hurt you, Kathleen," he said gently, in hopes of reassuring her.

With her back to him, she shook her head. "Please leave, Ross," she said, her voice broken by tears. "I can't bear this now. Please."

Ross knew what it felt like to be shut out. It was something he'd been experiencing all his life. But being shut out by Kathleen was something altogether different. As he went out the door, there was an ache in his heart such as he'd never known.

* * *

The next morning Kathleen had to drag herself out of bed. She felt dead, physically and emotionally dead. After Ross had left the house she'd cried a storm of tears, and finally, when no more tears would come, she'd lain awake in the dark, thinking and hurting, agonizing over every word Ross had said to her and regretting every word she'd said to him.

He hadn't deserved the outburst she'd laid on him. He was only trying to help her get Stormy. He didn't know that Kathleen had fallen in love with him. And last night, when he'd proposed, that love had gotten tangled up in everything he was saying and everything she was feeling.

He must be thinking she was a hysterical wreck of a woman, she thought with a groan of self-disgust. But when he'd talked about a marriage of convenience, Kathleen's heart had been torn right down the middle. She didn't want that from him. She wanted more. But she was going to have to forget all of that. She was going to have to completely forget this whole marriage thing.

She couldn't marry Ross. Living with him under the same roof would make it impossible for her to keep her true feelings hidden. And when he discovered that Kathleen loved him, he'd feel caught, maybe even obliged to stay in the marriage. No, she couldn't have that. It would be like reliving her nightmare of a marriage to Greg all over again. Ross didn't love her, and sooner or later he would find a woman he did love and want to have children with. And then she'd have to let him go.

Kathleen had just finished giving Stormy a bath and had dressed her in a pair of footed pajamas when the telephone rang. As she hurried to answer it, she realized she wanted it to be Ross's voice she heard on the other end of the line.

To her surprise, it was the police sergeant she and Ross had talked to about Stormy.

"What can I do for you this morning, Sergeant?" she asked quickly.

"I'm calling to tell you that we've found the person who left the baby on Mr. Douglas's porch."

Kathleen couldn't contain her gasp of surprise. "Who was it? Was it someone local?" Her heart began to race with dread. "What about the mother?"

"I think, Mrs. Hayes, it would be best if you'd come down to the precinct this morning. As soon as possible. We'll answer your questions then, okay?"

Kathleen was suddenly shaking with fear. Were they going to take the baby from her now? She needed Ross with her. "Yes, all right. I'll . . . be there shortly."

A week ago, Ross had been looking forward to getting back in the classroom, but this morning, his first day on the job, had been especially rough for him. Not because of rowdy or lethargic students, but rather from his lack of concentration. With half his thoughts on Kathleen, he couldn't make a lecture on American history interesting to a class of teenagers.

He feared his marriage proposal to Kathleen had driven a wedge between them, one that he might not ever be able to tear down. But Ross couldn't think about that now. He had another class in thirty minutes. He planned to lecture them on the Monroe Doctrine, and he didn't intend to have students leave the room yawning.

A click of high heels on hard tile caught his attention and he turned his head toward the doorway, expecting it to be a fellow teacher coming to welcome him aboard. Instead, he was shocked to see Kathleen walking into his room.

"I hope I'm not interrupting. The principal said I could probably find you here," she said.

He shook his head, thinking how gorgeous she looked. She was dressed in a black coat dress that buttoned all the way down to her knees with large gold buttons. A black-and-gold patterned scarf had been twisted, then tied around her head to hold her black hair away from her face.

Ross realized her beauty stunned him almost as much as her being here. Then he realized something else. The baby wasn't with her. "Where's Stormy?" he asked quickly. "They haven't taken her, have they?"

She held up her hand to allay his fears. "No. She's with Mother at the farmhouse."

She walked farther into the room, and Ross rose to his feet as her shaken state became apparent to him.

"Is something wrong, Kathleen?"

"I don't know. I mean, yes. It is."

He waited for her to go on. When she didn't, he skirted around the desk and took her by the arm. "Kathleen, you're pale and you're shaking like a leaf. Has something happened?"

Funny, she thought, how just hearing Ross's voice was enough to make her feel better. She looked up at him and tried her best to smile. "First of all, I want to apologize to you for last night. I said some awful things to you. Things that I know aren't true. You aren't like Greg. God forgive me for ever saying you were."

He reached out and touched her cheek. "You don't have to say this to me, Kathleen."

"Yes, I do. Because I don't want to hurt you. And I don't want you to be angry with me."

He groaned at the thought. Angry was the last thing he could ever be with Kathleen. "If you came all the way down here to ask me not to be angry with you, then you've wasted your time. I wasn't angry with you last night. I'm not angry with you now."

His voice grew soft on the last words, and Kathleen was suddenly reminded of that same low voice telling her he wanted to make love to her. It had sent shivers down her spine then, just like it was doing now.

"I'm glad about that, at least," she said, then sighed and passed a shaky hand across her brow. "I just came from the police station. They found the person who left Stormy on your porch."

Ross grabbed both her shoulders. "Who was it? Have they locked him or her behind bars?"

Her expression grim, Kathleen nodded. "Yes. But I don't really see what good locking him behind bars is going to do now."

"Him? It was the father? What a bastard!"

"No, it wasn't the father of the baby, although I think he did know about it. But since he didn't want any part of the child, it didn't matter to him what they did with it." Feeling her knees growing spongy, she reached for his arm. "I'm sorry, Ross, I've got to sit down."

Ross led her over to a long wooden bench next to a plate glass window. Sunlight streamed down on them and bathed Kathleen's pale face with warmth. Ross waited patiently while she drew in several long breaths and tried to collect herself.

"Actually," she told him, "it was the grandfather who left the child. Apparently the whole family is poor and uneducated. A daughter became pregnant out of wedlock, and since she was far too young to be able to keep the baby, they decided to give it away."

Ross's head shook back and forth as though he couldn't believe what he was hearing. "But why? And why give it to me?"

"That part is—" unable to stop herself, she clutched at his hands "—I think the strangest and saddest part of all. None of them wanted the baby. They all considered her just another mouth to feed. But the mother wanted me to have her."

Ross was stunned. "You! It was someone who knew you?"

Kathleen shrugged, as though she were just as lost as he was about the whole thing. "I scarcely remember the girl, Ross. From what I can recall, she was in a reading class of mine. And I do remember that she would only show up for school maybe two days out of the week. I tried to give her special attention. I guess she must have remembered that, I don't know. Anyway, she told the police that her father had meant to take the baby to my house, but apparently he got the houses mixed up and she wound up on your porch."

"Oh Lord, this is unbelievable!"

Kathleen nodded. "I know. Unbelievable and sad."

He looked at her as new thoughts struck him. "So what does this all mean? What's going to happen to Stormy?"

"The girl and her parents have signed all rights to the child over to the state. She'll be placed on an adoption list."

"And that terrifies you, doesn't it?" he asked softly.

She nodded, her eyes brimming with tears. "You can't imagine how much," she whispered.

A tear rolled onto her cheek and Ross wiped it away with the pad of his thumb. He wanted to help her. He'd do anything to make her happy, if only she'd let him. "That's why we should get married, Kathleen. If the courts saw us as two parents, a mother and a father, then the chances of us getting her would be far greater. You know that."

She knew a lot of things. Mainly that she couldn't marry this man, even at the risk of losing Stormy. Rising shakily to her feet, she said, "I know, Ross. But I haven't changed my mind."

Groaning with frustration, Ross pushed his fingers through his hair. What was he going to do? What could he say to her to make her see reason?

A group of teenagers was now milling about in the hall outside the classroom. Seeing them, Kathleen figured lunch hour was nearly over and the bell was about to ring. "I'd better go," she said.

"Kathleen, we've got to talk about this," he said, desperately catching her arm as she turned to go.

Her eyes pleading with him, she shook her head. "It's wrong. It's all wrong, Ross."

There was nothing wrong with loving her and wanting to marry her. But how could he tell her that when she was so obviously embittered over her past? She didn't want his love. She didn't want to be his wife. All she wanted was the baby. It was something he'd known from the very beginning, but that didn't make it hurt any less.

Suddenly the bell rang and students began to pour into the room. Ross was forced to release his hold on Kathleen's arm. The minute he did, she shot out of the room, leaving him no opportunity to say anything else to her.

It was just as well, he thought dismally, as he turned back to his desk and began to gather up his history notes. Right now he didn't know what to do or say that would make a difference between them. Maybe he never would.

Chapter Eleven

When Kathleen returned to the farmhouse to pick up Stormy, the whole family was amazed to hear what she'd learned at the police station. They were also concerned about Kathleen's growing involvement with the baby and afraid of what it might do to her if she lost her.

None of them was more worried than Sam, who followed his sister out to the car as she prepared to leave.

"Kathleen, why don't you spend the night with us?" he suggested as he handed the baby over to her.

She smiled wanly as she took Stormy from him and strapped her safely in the car seat. Sam had always been her protector. Anytime she'd ever been in trouble or needed help she'd been able to come to him, and he would do anything humanly possible to help her. But this time she was afraid there was nothing anyone could do.

She'd made the mistake of falling in love with a man she couldn't have and a baby she couldn't keep. How could anyone possibly help her?

As she settled herself behind the steering wheel, she looked up at her brother. "I don't think so, Sam. I need to be home in case the child-welfare people try to get in touch with me."

"Do you think that will be soon?" he asked, shutting the car door, then leaning his head into the open window.

She nodded glumly. "I'm afraid so. Parker Montgomery said the temporary custody would only last a few days at the most. Or until a foster home could be found. I'm sure I'll have to turn her over in the next few days."

He placed his hand on her shoulder. "Kathleen, I can't stand to see you so torn up like this."

Kathleen pressed the heels of her palms against her aching eyes. "This might be my only chance of ever having a baby. Oh, Sam, I'm terrified of losing her." She dropped her hands and looked back at her brother's worried face. "Ross has asked me to marry him. He says it might help my chances of adopting Stormy."

Sam didn't say anything for a moment and Kathleen watched his face for a reaction. However, with her brother it was always hard to tell what he was thinking. The only thing about his expression that changed was the faint arch of one dark brow.

"It probably would," he said after several moments had passed. "What did you tell him?"

His question had Kathleen gasping audibly. "What do you mean, what did I tell him? Good Lord, Sam, you know I had to say no!"

"Why? Because of what Greg did to you?"

It was true that her bad marriage to Greg had left her wounded and scarred, and more than a little wary of men and marriage. Yet Kathleen knew the biggest reason she couldn't marry Ross was because she loved him. But Kathleen couldn't tell her brother that. What she felt for Ross was too fresh, too private and precious a thing to share with anyone.

"Isn't that reason enough?" she answered.

He frowned. "What are you going to do, let his memory ruin your entire life?"

Anxious now to end their conversation, Kathleen put her hand on the key. "It's not that simple, Sam. Believe me."

He gave a lock of her hair an affectionate tug. "Just remember, sis, that I know what it's like to suffer. I lived my own private kind of hell until Olivia came back from Africa. We all need someone to love us. You included."

Yes, she did need someone to love her, Kathleen thought as she drove home. But she couldn't make Ross love her, anymore than she could marry him just for legal purposes.

When Ross arrived home from school, he drove straight to Kathleen's, only to find she wasn't home.

Frustrated, he went back to his own house and told himself to calm down. Even if she had been home, Ross doubted he could have reasoned with her any better than he had earlier today.

Still, he couldn't shake this helpless, desperate feeling that had settled over him, as if a bomb were tied to him and was ticking away. If he didn't do something to stop it from exploding, he would lose Kathleen, they'd lose the baby, and the family he wanted so badly would be lost to him forever.

For the next hour Ross paced the house and watched the highway for the sight of Kathleen's car. When he finally spotted it, he threw on his jacket and hurried out to his truck.

Kathleen had just gotten into the house and placed Stormy on the couch when she heard Ross's pickup pull into the driveway. As she went to the door to let him in, her heart leaped in spite of the misgivings she had about being with him.

"May I come in?" he asked.

How could she turn him away when everything inside her ached to be with him? She pushed the door wider and stood aside to allow him entry.

"I just got home," she told him, noticing he was still wearing the jeans and boots he'd been wearing at school, but his tweed sports coat had been replaced with the well-worn letter jacket, a garment she was beginning to associate with him.

"I know. I've been watching for you," he said.

As Ross moved into the room, he spotted the baby on the couch. It was a relief to see her again and he took her out of her carrier and held her close to his chest.

Kathleen didn't say anything. She was too busy watching him with the baby. It was obvious he loved her, and Kathleen wondered if the real reason Ross wanted to marry her was so he would have the chance to be Stormy's father.

"You were watching for me," she repeated. "Why? Was there some reason you needed to see me? Did the police contact you about anything?"

With his hand carefully cradling the baby's head, he lifted her against his shoulder and pressed his cheek against hers. She smelled powdery soft and sweet and innocent. He'd never known that babies smelled that way. He'd never known he could feel such fierce protectiveness toward such a tiny being. He'd never dreamed he would ever want to be a daddy. But he did. He wanted it almost as much as he wanted Kathleen to be his wife.

"No. They've probably tied up all the loose ends of the case by now," he told her.

"Then why did you want to see me?"

He put the baby back on the couch, but she immediately began to cry, so he picked her up again.

"I imagine she's hungry," Kathleen said as she went to her diaper bag for a bottle. "I'll go heat this and be right back."

A couple of minutes later, Kathleen returned with the warmed bottle. Ross took it and settled himself and Stormy in one of the armchairs.

While Ross gave Stormy her bottle, Kathleen went to the kitchen and prepared a pot of fresh coffee and a tray of sandwiches. She wasn't hungry, but she figured he was. And she needed something to keep her busy and away from him as much as possible.

"You didn't have to do that for me," he said, motioning his head toward the sandwiches she'd prepared.

Kathleen glanced around to see Ross had entered the kitchen. Nervously, she reached for a tea towel and wiped her hands. "I figured you hadn't eaten anything this evening. Have you?"

He shook his head. He'd been too wired up to eat. "I didn't come up here to have you fix me something to eat."

She carried the sandwiches over to the breakfast bar. "I didn't expect you did," she said, then looked at him as he took a seat on the bar stool next to her. "Where's Stormy?"

"She's asleep. I put her on your bed. And yes, I covered her up and put pillows beside her," he added before she had the chance to ask.

"You remembered," she said quietly, her green eyes going soft as she looked into his face.

"I remember a lot more than you think," he said in a low voice.

Kathleen remembered, too. She recalled every moment she'd spent in his arms. She remembered the rough texture of his hands against her skin, the eager warmth of his lips. She remembered every sigh, every kiss, every word he'd said to her.

It was all burned into her mind. As though he'd branded his mark on her without ever fully possessing her. The thoughts caused heat to seep to the surface of her cheeks, forcing her to look away from him.

She handed him a mug full of coffee. "I told my family what the police had to say. And I talked to Parker Montgomery about it."

Ross took a bite of sandwich, but for all he knew he was chewing wood chips. "And what did he have to say?"

Still unable to meet his eyes, she shrugged. "He can't really give me any kind of reassurance. Though he does know my temporary custody will end any day now."

She sounded resigned to the fact, which only made Ross want to reach over and shake her. "That's why we can't wait around about this, Kathleen. We have to get married. Now, tomorrow, or as quickly as we can!"

Kathleen didn't answer him. Instead, she stared unseeingly at the other end of the room and wondered what her life would be like once Stormy and Ross were no longer in it.

"Kathleen? Did you hear what I said?"

She turned her head to look at him, and as she did, she tried to steel her heart against him. "Ross, why are you badgering me about this? I told you no, and I meant it. I'm not going to marry you. Not now. Not ever."

Tossing down the sandwich, he wearily scrubbed his face with both hands. "Then all I can say is you must not want Stormy very badly."

Kathleen wanted to strike at him with both her fists, to scream how wrong he was. But all she could manage to do was stare at him as a chilling pain swept over her.

"How dare you say that to me! You could never know how much that baby means to me," she said in a low, fierce voice. "You could never know how much I want her!"

All the doubts and uncertainty she'd felt these past few days suddenly welled up in her throat, choking her with fear. With a strangled sob, she slipped off the bar stool and ran out of the room before he had a chance to stop her.

A few moments later, Ross found her in one of the spare bedrooms. She was sitting on the side of the bed with her back to him. Her shoulders were slumped, her head bent downward. When he sat beside her and lifted her face to his, he found tears on her cheeks.

The sight of them cut him to the core and he wanted more than anything to draw her into his arms and kiss them away.

"I'm sorry, Kathleen. Maybe I was wrong—"

"You were wrong!"

His hands lifted, then fell helplessly back to his knees. "I don't understand you, Kathleen."

She began to quiver like a trapped animal doomed to a fate it couldn't control. "No, you can't understand, Ross. Because you don't know. And if you did you could see why I do want Stormy so badly."

Reaching out, he cupped the side of her face. "Then tell me, Kathleen. This is tearing me up. I want to help you, but I don't know how."

Something in his voice prompted her to look at him and as she did she realized that she could no longer think just about herself, her feelings and wants. She had to think about Ross and what all of this was doing to him. "The reason I—" With a shake of her head, she stopped, then started again. "The truth is, Ross, I can't have children."

Ross felt as if he'd been whacked in the chest and had lost his air. Kathleen. His beautiful Kathleen, unable to have children? He couldn't believe it! He didn't want to believe it!

"Kathleen, I...dear God, why didn't you tell me?"

Amazed that he had to ask why, Kathleen's eyes searched his face. "Because I couldn't! Because I didn't want you to know! Do you think it's something a woman is proud to announce? Something she can go around telling a man who—" She broke off abruptly, appalled at what she'd been about to say. A *man who she loves*. She'd almost told Ross that she loved him!

Drawing in a desperate breath, she turned her head away and stared across the bedroom, which was quickly becoming dark now that the sun had set.

"Kathleen, look at me," he said, his thumb and forefinger dragging her chin back around to him. "Didn't I make it clear that you could tell me anything?"

She nodded stiffly as she recalled the conversation they'd shared over dinner on New Year's Day.

"Well, that means anything and everything." His hold on her chin eased, but his fingers remained on her face, to gently trace her cheek. "I would have understood. I understand now," he said softly.

His touch and his kindness brought a bittersweet ache to Kathleen's heart. "I'm glad you understand, Ross. So now you can see why I can't marry you."

Bewildered, he shook his head. "No, I don't see that. You not being able to bear children shouldn't stop you from marrying me. It should make you want to marry me even more—seeing that Stormy might be the only child you'll have."

"Might have," she reminded him wearily, then rose to her feet and walked across the room. A framed picture of Sam, Nick and herself was sitting atop a dresser just to her right. She picked it up and studied it for long minutes before she said, "You're not thinking about this, Ross. Not really thinking."

He went across the room to stand at her shoulder. "And you're thinking too much," he told her.

Her head twisted up and around in order to see his face. "One of us needs to. I've already gone through this once, Ross. Greg wanted a family. I don't really know why—he wasn't a family-type man. Maybe it was an ego thing, I don't know. And I guess that part of it no longer matters. What does matter is that I couldn't give him one, and he became very unhappy in our marriage."

"Kathleen—" he began, only to have her interrupt.

"Don't tell me it doesn't matter, Ross. Because I know that it does! I know how dissatisfied and trapped he felt by our marriage. And it would be the same way with you."

He lifted her long hair in his hands, relishing the silky texture and the flowery scent that rose to his senses. "It wouldn't be the same at all. I'm not asking you to marry me to give me children. I don't expect you to give me any."

Jut having Ross so close to her, having his chest brushing against her shoulders, his hands in her hair, made her nearly weep with longing. She knew he desired her physically, and she knew all she would have to do to have him was to turn and invite him into her arms.

But she knew in the end a physical relationship between them would only complicate matters even more. And a marriage based solely on physical desire would be even worse than marrying to adopt Stormy.

"I know that you only want a marriage of convenience," she said, her voice growing thick. "But what if you fell in love with someone and wanted to have children with her? Do you know how guilty that would make me feel?"

How could he tell her that her fears were groundless? How could he tell her that he would never fall in love with someone else because he'd already fallen in love with her? And that he would love her forever? He couldn't.

More than likely she would think he was making it up just to allay her fears. But on the other hand, if she did believe him, he had no doubts that she would run as fast and as far away from him as she could possibly get.

Groaning at the hopelessness of it all, he said, "Kathleen, you're getting way ahead of yourself. Besides, if that should ever happen, we could get a divorce. Like I first suggested."

She whirled on him, her face rigid with anger. "That would really be nice, wouldn't it," she hurled at him. "Give Stormy two parents and let her get used to having both a mother and a father, then get a divorce and split her family apart. How could I explain that to her? Tell her that she wasn't important enough? That her daddy had to move on and make himself another family?"

Ross wanted to curse at the top of his lungs. But rather than give in to the urge, he drew in a steadying breath and said, "It wouldn't be like that, Kathleen."

Shaking from head to toe, she stepped around him. "This is it, Ross! I'm not discussing this any further. In fact, I'd prefer it if I never saw you again!"

Ross stared at her retreating back, knowing he couldn't have felt any more pain if she'd pushed a lance right through his heart.

"What about Stormy? You'd keep me from seeing her?"

At the doorway to the bedroom, she turned and looked back at him. She saw the raw pain on his face and realized how much she was hurting this man, and she hated it. But she was doing it out of love. She had to keep telling herself that, or she was going to shatter into a thousand pieces.

"No. I wouldn't do that. You can see her whenever you want. But this—this thing between us is over. Don't ever mention the word marriage to me again!"

"Okay, class, tomorrow we're going to be discussing amending the Constitution. Who can tell me what the first ten amendments to the constitution are called?"

Ross turned away from the blackboard to see several hands raised in the air. He pointed to a blond-headed girl in the back.

"The Bill of Rights, Mr. Douglas," she answered.

"That's right, Cynthia," he said, then turned back to the blackboard and began to write. "So, your assignment for tomorrow, class, is to write a brief description of each amendment that makes up our Bill of Rights."

The bell rang and noise filled the room as students called to each other and made a quick race to the door.

Ross was gathering up a stack of papers to take home to grade when he realized someone had returned to the room. Looking up, he saw it was one of his history students.

"Did you forget something, Matthew?"

"No, Mr. Douglas," he said, taking a tentative step toward Ross. "I just wanted to ask you—well, the rumor has been going around school that when you played baseball in college, a major-league team offered you a contract."

Apparently Matthew was going to be one of his baseball players, he thought wryly. "Well, I don't know where you heard the rumor, but it's true."

The tall, lanky boy was obviously impressed. "Wow! So why aren't you still playing? I mean, you're not too old to play baseball."

Smiling, Ross dropped a friendly hand on the boy's shoulder. "No, I'm not too old. I had a knee injury. That's fatal for a guy who plays catcher."

"So you had to retire," Matthew said, his expression as miserable as if he'd suffered the injury himself. "I guess teaching must be boring after playing in a minor-league club."

Ross chuckled. "It's not boring at all. I enjoy making sure boys like you know what the Bill of Rights is."

"Aw, shoot. Is that really the truth?"

"It's really the truth," he told the boy. And it was the truth, Ross realized. Teaching wasn't just something he'd taken up because he could no longer play baseball. It was what he wanted to do with his life. He wanted to be with children. To try to make a difference in their lives. There were too many of them out there with only one parent or no parents at all. He wanted to be there for as many of them as he could be. He wanted to see that his students never felt as left out as he had.

"Boy, you must really like kids," Matthew said.

When Ross left the building a few minutes later, he was still thinking about Matthew's comments. The boy's words had made him realize just how much he did like kids. Even though he'd always told himself he liked his freedom better.

However, that had all changed when he'd found Stormy on his front porch. In spite of his fears about marriage, he wanted to be Stormy's father. And he couldn't be Stormy's father unless he married Kathleen and they tried to adopt her together. But he could hardly see that happening now. Kathleen didn't care if he ever showed his face in her life again. In fact, she would probably be happy if he didn't.

Well, he thought grimly, he'd left her alone last night, although it had very nearly killed him to stay away. But tonight he was going up to see her and the baby. He wouldn't mention marriage. But he would let Kathleen know that he hadn't forgotten about it, either.

"Ross?"

At the sound of his name, Ross turned to see Nick Gallagher jogging toward him.

"Nick! How on earth did you find me here?"

"I remembered you telling Mom and Dad where you'd be teaching. Are you on your way home?"

Ross nodded, wondering why Kathleen's brother had gone to the trouble of looking him up. "Is... something wrong? Has something happened to Kathleen?"

Nick shook his head, but from the frown on his face Ross could see something *was* wrong.

"It's not—she hasn't had an accident or anything. But she's in awful shape, Ross. She had to turn the baby over today. A child-welfare worker took Stormy to a foster home."

Ross felt like he'd been hit with an ax. "Where is she now?" he asked, a sick feeling in the pit of his stomach.

"You mean Kathleen?"

Ross nodded soberly.

"She's at the farm. She was so torn up, Dad wouldn't let her drive home." He made a helpless gesture with his hand. "I thought if you'd come over to the farm and see her, it might help."

Ross was more than surprised at Nick's request. "I, uh, don't think Kathleen wants to see me. She didn't ask to see me, did she?"

Nick frowned. "No. But right now Kathleen doesn't know what she's doing or saying. She only knows her baby has been taken away from her."

Lifting his face to the sky, Ross drew in a long breath in hopes of easing the pain in his chest. "This is all my fault. If it wasn't for me, Kathleen wouldn't be in this shape now!"

Nick folded his arms. "You sound about as crazy as Kathleen does. It isn't your fault she wants that baby so badly. Didn't you know about...well, Kathleen can't have children."

"I know. She told me."

Nick couldn't keep his surprise hidden. Ross could see his shock and realized that other than the family, Kathleen hadn't told anybody about her inability to conceive. Until now. Ross thought about that as Nick continued, "Then you can understand why she's hurting so badly."

"I do understand. I just can't see that I could do anything about it. I tried." He groaned with frustration. "Oh, hell, I should never have taken the baby up to Kathleen's house that night. I should have gotten her down the mountain somehow."

Nick slung his arm around Ross's shoulder. "You did the best you could for the baby. Don't be feeling guilty now. Just come talk to Kathleen."

"She has all of you, Nick. You're her family."

"Yes, she has all of us. But you're the one she needs."

No one had ever needed Ross. It was incredible to him to think that Kathleen did.

"I do want to see her," Ross admitted.

"Good." Nick gave his shoulder an encouraging shake. "She doesn't know I came over here to find you and I won't tell her you're coming. But I can tell you that the whole family is going to give a sigh of relief when they see you."

"Why is that?"

Nick's expression was suddenly wry. "Can't you see that Kathleen loves you? We all can."

Chapter Twelve

Kathleen loves you. Kathleen loves you. As he drove to the Gallagher farm, the words played over and over in his head like a litany he couldn't shut off.

Could Nick be right? Did Kathleen love him? She'd responded to him physically, but she wouldn't make love with him. Moreover, she completely refused to marry him. That didn't sound to Ross like a woman in love.

When Ross arrived at the farmhouse, Nick met him at the door and led him through the kitchen and into the den.

Olivia, Allison and Ella were all sitting on the couch going over brides' magazines. Kathleen was sitting on the floor with Benjamin, who was showing her the new eyes Ella had sewn on the stuffed basset hound Kathleen had given him.

"I'm sure Buddy can see a rabbit a mile off with those eyes," Kathleen told the boy.

Ben giggled. "Will he chase the rabbit and eat him?"

Kathleen smiled wanly. "Buddy only chases rabbits. He'll come home and eat dog food for his supper."

Benjamin giggled again. "Buddy won't do that, Kathleen, 'cause he don't eat dog food."

"Ben," Nick called out fondly, "come here, son. Let's go with Uncle Sam to feed the hogs."

Always ready to go with Nick, Ben jumped to his feet and followed Nick out of the room. The three women on the couch rose to their feet also.

"Girls, I think it's about time we started supper," Ella said. "And S.T. wants ribs tonight. We'd better cook up some barbecue sauce."

Ross hardly noticed as the women quietly filed out of the room. He was too busy looking at Kathleen, who was still sitting on the floor, staring up at him.

He moved closer, and as he did, Ross could see that she'd been crying long and hard. Her face and eyes were swollen, her hair disheveled. She looked terribly sad, and terribly beautiful.

"What are you doing here?" she asked him.

"I heard about Stormy," he said quietly.

She looked away from him and Ross knew she was struggling to keep more tears from surfacing.

"You shouldn't have come. There's nothing you can do."

Her voice was flat, as though every bit of life had drained out of her. Ross realized she didn't want to see him. All she wanted was to get her baby back. It was a painful fact. Nick might know all about Allison's heart, but he didn't know about his sister's. She didn't love Ross. He'd been crazy to ever hope she would.

He'd been even crazier to think he could compete with Stormy and the Gallagher family for her affection.

"It's not over, Kathleen. She hasn't been adopted. She's only gone to a foster home." He knelt beside her, trying to comfort her.

She looked back at him and her face crumpled as fresh tears filled her eyes. "They just took her, Ross. Like it was nothing. They took *our* baby! She was mine and yours, not theirs. She belongs to us!"

Ross drew her into his arms and pressed her cheek against his chest. "I know, Kathleen. It hurts me, too," he said, his voice rough with emotion.

Sobs were torn from her throat as she buried her face in the folds of his shirt and clung to him desperately. For long moments Ross stroked her hair and back and prayed for her tears to subside. He couldn't bear for her to be hurting this way. And though he'd never believed himself capable of loving any woman, he knew Kathleen meant more to him than his very life.

Eventually Kathleen pulled away from him and wiped her eyes with the back of her hands. She hadn't meant to break down in front of Ross. But the moment she'd looked up and seen him, she'd been struck by how much he'd become a part of her life. She'd been struck by the memory of him carrying Stormy into the house that first night. He'd been half-frozen and covered with snow. But his only thoughts and concern had been for the baby. She'd loved him for that. And for so many more reason, she loved him now.

That was why her heart was breaking. She not only had to give up Stormy today, she knew she had to give up Ross, as well. He was a man who deserved to have children of his own. And since she couldn't give him any, she wanted him to be free to marry someone who could.

"I'm sorry," she said, rising to her feet and pushing her tousled hair out of her face. "I didn't mean to get so emotional. I guess you think... I'm one of the weakest women you've ever seen."

"I don't think you're weak. I think you're human."

Swallowing the lump in her throat, she turned and walked over to the fireplace. She couldn't remain close to Ross, otherwise she might just fling herself into his arms. "Yes, well, I don't feel very human now. I feel dead inside."

Her defeated expression had Ross slowly shaking his head. "Kathleen, you can't give up now. You can't just say it's over, they took her and I'll never get her back. We've got to fight to get her back. The real mother wanted you to have her. Maybe there's a way she could simply sign the baby over to you."

Kathleen shook her head. "I don't think so. The mother is a minor. And even if she wasn't, I'm sure I'd still have to go through adoption procedures to get her."

"We're going to get her," he said firmly.

Her hands lifted, then fell back to her sides. "And how do you propose to do that, Ross? There's no telling how many couples are out there on a waiting list. Waiting for a newborn like Stormy to come along. My name will be way down at the bottom."

Fresh determination made Ross go to her and take her by the arm. "We had Stormy first. We were the ones who rescued her in that ice storm—that should count for something. We can talk to that lawyer of yours and tell him that we're going to be married. We can let him and the child-welfare department see how much we want her!''

Anger gave Kathleen the strength to jerk her arm away from his grasp. ''I told you not to ever mention that word to me again! How could you . . . bring it up now? What are you trying to do, rip me completely apart?''

It was obvious that he'd angered her. But Ross didn't care. Anger was much better than tears. And now was the time for her to see how things really were, not after it was too late to do anything.

''You keep telling me how much you want the baby. So why don't you prove it? Why don't you quit trying to hide behind a bunch of excuses and prove how much you want her?''

Incredulous, Kathleen opened her mouth to protest. ''I don't have to prove anything!'' she spluttered, her eyes suddenly snapping with fire. ''And I'm not trying to hide behind anything, either!''

''Yes, you are! You have all sorts of reasons and excuses not to marry me. But we both know they're not the real reason you're fighting me!''

Everything inside of her went stock-still. Did he know? Had he guessed that she loved him? She looked away from him and into the fire. ''What are you saying?''

''I'm saying that you don't want to marry me because you're too afraid.''

''I'm not afraid! I'm—''

His hands closed around her shoulders, forcing her to turn her head and look at him. ''Don't lie to me, Kathleen. The fear of living is more frightening to you than the fear of losing Stormy.''

"That's not true!" she cried, her whole body beginning to tremble.

His fingers bit into her shoulders as frustration drove him on. "It is true, Kathleen. When you look at me and Stormy, all you can think about is your husband and the baby you couldn't give him. You're not really thinking about me, or her, or what might be best for us! You're thinking about yourself!"

Her eyes were suddenly hard green rocks. "You—you cruel bastard!"

Before Ross realized what he was doing, he'd jerked her into his arms and captured her lips with his.

Instinctively, Kathleen raised her hands to push him away, but by the time they reached his chest, the anger inside her had been swept away by his kiss. Her fingers curled into his shirt, her lips clung mindlessly to his.

Ross had to force himself to tear his lips away from hers. "Goodbye, Kathleen. When you decide what it is you really want, you know where to find me."

Kathleen watched him walk away, wondering how long it would take for this ache in her heart to subside. And wondering, too, how long, if ever, it would take her to forget him.

"Kathleen, what do you think about this one?"

Kathleen looked at the pearl pink dress Olivia had zipped Allison into and tried her best to look interested. "It's pretty. But it's too glamorous for a wedding."

Frowning, Olivia went over and pulled Kathleen off the dressing-room chair. "All right, you came with us to be a help. So you're going to help, not sit there on your butt and mope."

"I'm not moping," Kathleen argued with her sis-
er-in-law.

"She is, isn't she, Allison?"

The youngest of the three women nodded in agreement. "I'm afraid you are, Kathleen. You haven't said
more than three sentences since we came into this
ridal shop."

Olivia shook her head. "I thought you were excited
bout Nick and Allison's wedding."

"I am. I couldn't be more thrilled about it. Allison
nows that."

"Well," Olivia said, throwing her hands up in the
ir, "then act like it. The wedding is on Valentine's
Day, remember? That gives us only a short time to get
verything ready. And we've got to find the perfect
ress, one that will knock Nick right off his feet the
moment he sees Allison in it."

"That shouldn't be too hard. Nick is still walking on
ir."

Allison shook her head and Olivia groaned.

"Okay, I'll try to have a bit more enthusiasm, if
hat's what you two want," Kathleen said. She gave
hem a broad smile. "There. Is that better?"

"It would be if it were real," Olivia told her.

Sighing, Allison stepped out of the pink dress.
Maybe I should just wear the dress Nick bought me.
The one I wore at your wedding, Olivia."

Kathleen felt awful. She loved Allison and wanted
er to have a wonderful wedding, but it was hard to
ut on a happy face when she felt dreadful. "Don't be
lly. You deserve a beautiful wedding dress." She went
o Allison and put her arm around her shoulders.
Don't mind my moodiness, Allison."

The younger woman put her hand on Kathleen
cheek. "We only want you to be happy."

"Yes, I know. And I will be. Just give me a litt
time, that's all I need. But for right now I'm goir
back out to the front to see if I can't find you anothe
dress to try on."

As soon as Kathleen stepped out of the dressin
room, Olivia and Allison exchanged worried looks.

"We've got to do something about this," Oliv
said.

Allison nodded grimly. "You're right. But what?

The women did find a wedding dress. It was mac
of antique ivory lace with a high collar and leg-o
mutton sleeves. The romantic style suited Alliso
beautifully, as did the color, which was a perfect fc
for her tawny red hair.

Pleased with their success, the women decided
splurge on lunch at a nearby restaurant that serve
delicious Mexican food.

"I miss Nick so much since he had to go back
Fort Sill," Allison said.

The three women were sitting at a booth by th
window, sharing a basket of tortilla chips and sal
while they waited for the main course to be brought
them.

"I know you do," Olivia said. "But at least we no
know his transfer has come through and he'll be mo
ing back here to Fort Chaffee next month. Having hi
home to stay will be worth the wait."

Smiling, Allison nodded in agreement. "Gran
mother Lee was so happy to hear that we'll be livir
here. I think she would have missed Nick more tha
she would have missed me."

"We're all happy that you and Nick will be living close to us," Kathleen told her.

"Especially Sam," Olivia said. "He doesn't come out and say it, but I can tell that when Nick's not around, he misses him terribly." She glanced at Kathleen. "And he's also wondering why we haven't seen Ross lately. He'd like for him to come back over for supper one night this week."

Even though her heart lurched at the mention of Ross's name, she gave her sister-in-law an indifferent shrug. "I'm sure he would come if you'd give him a call. Just be sure and warn me so I won't be around."

Olivia made a snorting noise. "Kathleen, I'm tired of tiptoeing around you. So is Allison. So is the whole family. We understand that you've been upset about Stormy. But what about Ross? We want to know what happened between the two of you."

"Nothing has happened," Kathleen said, her eyes carefully avoiding the other two women. "Now that Stormy is gone there is no reason for us to be together."

Olivia glanced at Allison before turning her attention back to Kathleen. "How can you say that?"

"Because it's the truth," she said shortly.

"Sam said that Ross asked you to marry him."

Kathleen's hand trembled as she reached for her water glass. "Sam has a big mouth."

"Sam? A big mouth?" Olivia echoed wryly.

"Well, in this case he had one," Kathleen said, "because he shouldn't have told you about it."

Olivia sighed impatiently and Allison said, "We thought you were falling in love with Ross. Now you don't even want to see him."

"You're right. I don't want to see him. When I'm—" She had to stop. She couldn't tell them that every time she was in the same room with Ross it tore her apart. Reaching for a chip, she forced herself to continue, "Just believe me when I say it's best Ross and I don't... be with each other."

"Then you didn't care about Ross? You were just hanging around with him because of the baby," Olivia said.

"No, I..." An annoyed frown on her face, she looked at both women. "I don't have to explain my feelings about Ross to you two."

"No, you don't," Olivia agreed.

"But we care about you," Allison said. "And we know...well, you remember how mixed up and afraid I was when Nick asked me to marry him. You gave me the nudge I needed to make me see things clearly."

"And you surely haven't forgotten how miserable I was when I was trying to come to terms with my feelings for Sam. But even though I was miserable, you kept pushing me toward him anyway."

"Somebody had to," Kathleen said, a grimace on her face. "You didn't know your own mind. Neither did Allison."

"And you know your own mind about Ross?" Allison wanted to know.

Desperate to put an end to this interrogation, Kathleen leaned across the table toward the two women. "You both," she began in a quiet but fierce voice, "want to know how I really feel about Ross? I love him desperately. I'm miserable without him. But that's something I'm just going to have to learn to live with."

Allison shook her head in dismay, while Olivia let out a long, disappointed breath.

"Why?" Olivia asked.

Kathleen tried to ignore the pain in her heart. But it was impossible and it showed in her voice as she began to speak. "Ross doesn't love me. And even if he did, I wouldn't marry him."

"Very sensible," Olivia said with sarcasm. "It might make you happy and we can't have that. That would ruin your plans to be miserable for the rest of your life."

Kathleen kept her eyes fixed on the traffic outside the plate glass window. "You two think it's all so simple. And I guess it is to you. You each have a man who loves you."

"How do you know Ross doesn't love you?" Allison asked. "Have you asked him?"

"No. And I'm not going to. Because whether he loves me or not isn't the issue."

This brought looks of amazement to Allison and Olivia.

"Love isn't the issue?" Olivia repeated. "Come on, Kathleen, love is always the one and only real issue. Don't try to say it isn't."

"Okay," she said, realizing these two weren't going to stop unless she came out with everything. "I love Ross too much to marry him. You both know I can't have children. How could I do that to him? He's a young man. How could I take away his chances of ever having a family?"

Allison reached across the table and touched Kathleen's hand. "Maybe he'd rather have you."

Kathleen's throat was suddenly lodged with tears, making it impossible for her to speak.

After a moment Olivia said, "You know, when Sam asked me to marry him, he didn't turn around in the same breath and ask me if I could bear children. Women never really know if they'll be able to have children until they start trying to. And when a man truly loves a woman, that doesn't really matter to him."

Allison nodded in agreement. "I know I have Benjamin and that makes things a little different in my case. Still, Nick didn't ask me if I could bear more children. I know he would like them. But I know he would marry me even if I couldn't."

Before anything more could be said, a waitress arrived with their meal. The three women began to eat, and eventually the conversation drifted back to the preparations for Allison and Nick's wedding. Kathleen was relieved, but she remained torn by what Olivia and Allison had said about love and having children.

Maybe she was wanting and expecting things to be too perfect. Maybe if she agreed to marry Ross, he would eventually come to love her, and nothing would matter to him except that they be together. It was more than her weary heart could dare to hope for.

Chapter Thirteen

The following day brought cold, drizzling rain. The dreary weather matched Ross's mood, but he didn't let it interfere with baseball training. Out on the gym floor, he had the boys do a calisthenics routine that would get them into shape before spring weather arrived and they could take to the field.

"Why can't we play catch, coach?" one of the boys in the group called to him.

Ross shook his head. "No gloves or baseball for at least another week. The team that wins the state championship this year will be the team that's the strongest. And I intend for that team to be you guys, so back to work. Ten laps around the gym. Up and down the bleachers," he added, to the consternation of the already tired boys.

As Ross watched the group head to the bleachers, he noticed a familiar figure standing at the edge of the court. All sorts of thoughts ran through his head as he jogged over to him.

"Hello, Ross."

Ross reached for Sam's hand and shook it warmly. "Good to see you. What brings you to school? Decide you wanted to play a little baseball?"

Sam grinned. "Not if I have to do all that," he said, motioning toward the group of boys jogging tiredly around the gym.

Ross laughed. "They don't like it, either."

Sam's expression grew serious again and Ross knew this man hadn't come here to make small talk.

"I'm not going to take up your time, Ross," he said. "I just came by to see why you haven't been over to the farm this past week. We've all missed you."

All of them except Kathleen, he thought ruefully. "Getting settled into this new position has kept me busy."

Frowning, Sam said, "Look, I'm not going to beat around the bush here. And I don't want you to, either—"

"Has Kathleen heard anything about the baby?" Ross asked quickly before Sam could go on.

"No, I'm afraid not."

"So...how is she? Kathleen, I mean."

Sam looked at him thoughtfully. "She's miserable. That's why I'm here. I want to know how you really feel about my sister."

"Sam, I'm not coming over to the farm tonight, so just forget it," Kathleen told him over the telephone. "All I want to do is eat a salad and relax in front of the TV."

"You never watch TV."

"I am tonight," she lied.

"Kathleen, you're making me mad."

"You can get glad in the same shoes," she told him, then hung up the phone before he could say anything more.

Normally, Kathleen loved to spend time with her family, but this past week they'd been smothering her. She realized they were doing it out of love, but what they didn't know was that it made her sadder to be around them. Sam had Olivia. Nick had Allison. Her mother and father had each other. Kathleen didn't have anyone.

Maybe that was her own fault, she thought sadly. Maybe what Ross had said was true. Maybe she was still living in the past, afraid to face the future and take life's risks.

Every night for the past week, she'd stood at the living-room window and stared through the woods toward the lights in Ross's house. She'd wondered what he was doing and how he would react if she were to show up on his doorstep.

Tonight she was staring at them again, the now-familiar ache in her heart weighing her down. At first she'd been so distraught over losing Stormy that she hadn't realized the full extent of her love for Ross. But now, after a week without him, she knew that he meant more to her than anything.

The fact had her turning away from the window and reaching for her sweater. Damn the risks, she whispered fiercely. On New Year's Eve she'd toasted in the coming year with Ross and made a resolution to forget her painful past. Now was the time to meet that resolution.

* * *

Ross had never been a man who got nervous. But tonight, as he prepared to go to the Gallagher farm for supper, the thought of seeing Kathleen was tying his stomach into anxious knots.

He'd been hoping, praying that this past week had given her the time and space she needed to see that they belonged together. Yet Kathleen hadn't approached him with a phone call or a visit, and now Sam had asked Ross to go to her. He wasn't sure it was the right thing to do, but he was desperate to make her understand that he needed her in his life.

He was pulling on his boots when he heard a knock at the door. "Just a minute," he called, wondering who could possibly be wanting to see him at this time of the evening.

When he opened the door and found Kathleen on the porch, he stared at her in total surprise.

"Kathleen!"

Her throat was so tight with nerves, she was forced to swallow before she could speak. "Hello, Ross. May I come in?"

He pushed the storm door open so that she could enter the house.

"I guess I should have called first. Is your phone working now?"

She looked around the neat living room, then at him. He was dressed in a pair of jeans and boots, and a white shirt that was unbuttoned and hanging loosely against his chest.

"Yes, it's working now. They hooked it up yesterday," he said, carefully shutting the door behind him.

Kathleen walked to the middle of the room, then stood facing him, her hands clasped awkwardly behind her back. It looked as though he'd just showered. His hair was wet and she could smell the faint scent of after-shave on him.

He began to button his shirt while Kathleen's heart began to race. "I, uh—were you going out? I wouldn't want to keep you."

From her question, she couldn't have known he was going to be at her family's for dinner tonight. Nor did she look as though she was planning on being there. She was wearing old jeans, a cardigan and a pair of ragged-looking flats. Her hair was pulled back into a ponytail and her face was devoid of makeup. In that moment he realized she'd never looked more beautiful to him.

"You're not keeping me," he assured her.

Kathleen moistened her lips with the tip of her tongue. "I guess after I saw you at the farm—" Not knowing how to go on, she stopped and drew in a bracing breath. "I've missed you."

Ross stared down at her, afraid to hope that her feelings had changed toward him. "I've missed you, too," he said.

She looked at him, wondering, aching. "Why didn't you come see me? Tell me?"

"Because you told me you didn't ever want to see me again. Remember?"

She sighed, recalling the day she'd lost Stormy, and then, later, had argued fiercely with Ross about marrying him. She'd been in agony ever since.

"Yes, I remember. But I was hoping you'd realize I didn't really mean it," she said, her eyes dropping away from his.

He continued to look at her. "If you didn't really mean it, why did you say it?"

Her hands lifted helplessly, then fell back to her sides. "Because I was desperate. And like you said, I was afraid." She looked back up at him, and as her eyes roamed his dear, familiar face, she couldn't hold back her feelings any longer. "I was afraid to tell you the truth."

Tentatively, his fingers reached out and touched her cheek. "And what is the truth, Kathleen?"

"That I love you."

Ross had prayed to hear her say those words, but he'd never expected it to happen. Now that it had, he was momentarily stunned.

"Oh, my Lord," he whispered in wondrous disbelief.

Afraid to see the rejection on his face, Kathleen quickly whirled around and away from him. "Now you know why I've been fighting you so."

Bewildered, he put his hands on her shoulders. "No, I don't know why. If you love me..."

She steeled herself to turn her head and look at him. "When I realized how I felt about you, I knew I couldn't settle for a marriage of convenience. And since that's what you want, I—"

His fingers gripping her shoulders, he gave her a little shake. "Kathleen, I proposed a marriage of convenience because I figured that was the only way I could get you to accept."

She shook her head from side to side, as though she couldn't believe what he was saying. "But you said...Ross, that very first night we met, you told me how you never wanted to be married, that family life wasn't for you."

"You told me the same thing," he reminded her.

"I know. But I changed my mind."

"So did I," he said, then drew her into the circle of his arms. "The moment I realized I loved you."

Kathleen clung to him as her whirling thoughts tried to take in what he was saying. "You love me?"

"Like nothing or no one in my whole life."

"I thought you wanted to marry me just because of Stormy."

His arms tightened around her and he pressed his cheek against the top of her head. "I do want to marry you because of Stormy. And because I want you to be my wife. A real wife. A wife I can hold in my arms. A wife I can make love to, and share the rest of my life with. But I was afraid to tell you that, Kathleen. I've never really been a part of a family before. When my parents got divorced, they both shut me out of their lives. That's why I vowed I'd never get married and put myself or an innocent child in such a vulnerable position."

She lifted her head away from his chest, and as Ross looked at her, he could still see doubt in her eyes.

"I understand that, Ross, but . . . this is all happening so quickly. We haven't really known each other that long."

"I don't need more time to know how I feel about you. Kathleen, this past week without you has been hell for me. Don't tell me we don't belong together. I won't accept that."

Her hands came up and framed his face. "I'm afraid I'll disappoint you. I only have myself to give you."

"Kathleen, ever since you told me you couldn't have children, I've wanted to ask how come you're so certain? Has a doctor told you there's absolutely no chance that you might conceive?"

She shook her head. "The doctors could never find a reason why I couldn't conceive. But since I never did, I assumed that something had to be wrong."

"Something was wrong," Ross agreed, "with your husband. Or was he tested, too?"

Kathleen grimaced. "No. He wouldn't agree to a fertility test. I guess it was an ego thing with him."

Ross's eyes were suddenly filled with hopeful light. "If your husband wasn't tested and you checked out healthy, then who's to say that things might be different with you and me? Maybe *we* could have a child together."

She gripped his forearms, afraid to let herself believe or hope that what he was saying might be true. "Do you really think there's an outside chance that the problem could have been with Greg?"

"I think there's more than an outside chance."

She studied his face, her expression guarded. "Maybe so, Ross. But what if it doesn't happen? What if I can't give you a child? I don't think I could bear it if you thought less of me. You deserve children and—"

"You deserve children, too," he said, drawing her closer against him. "And if we manage to adopt Stormy, we'll have one and it will be wonderful. If we don't, we'll have each other. And that's all that really matters, my darling Kathleen. You and me, sharing the rest of our lives together."

Happy tears filled her eyes. "Olivia and Allison tried to tell me you would feel that way. I was afraid to believe them."

For the first time since Kathleen had entered the house, he let himself smile. "I can see I'm going to have two very smart sisters-in-law."

She smiled back at him, her face an expression of pure love. "And I'm going to have a wonderful husband for the rest of my life."

Leaning his forehead against hers, he said, "Stormy might not be with us now, but she brought us together, and I thank God for that."

"Oh, Ross," she whispered, circling her arms around his neck. "Kiss me. Now, this very minute."

He crushed her to him, hungrily kissing her lips, her face, her throat. Kathleen touched him as if she'd never let him go.

Suddenly headlights swept across the room, warning them that someone had pulled into the driveway. Frustrated, Kathleen pulled away from him.

Chuckling, he said, "I see my smart sisters-in-law have called in the recruits. It's Sam."

"Sam!" Kathleen burst out. "Oh, my! He must be hopping mad because I hung up on him. He wanted me to come over for supper tonight and now—"

"I know," he said with a sheepish grin. "That's where I was getting ready to go. Then you came and—"

She looked at him with surprise. "You were going to be at the farm tonight?"

Quickly, he went to her and held her in his arms. "Sam asked me to come. And I couldn't refuse. Not when I loved you."

Suddenly she was giggling. "Sam? A matchmaker? This is wonderful!"

He bent his head and kissed her lips. "It's pretty wonderful, all right," he whispered as a knock sounded on the door. "Do you think we should let him in and tell him that he was successful?"

Laughing, she reached for Ross's hand, and together they went to give her brother the news.

Epilogue

One year later, the Gallagher farmhouse was ablaze with lights and filled with music, food and laughter, and most of all, family and friends.

It was New Year's Eve and it was also Stormy Douglas's first birthday. However, at the moment the little black-haired, green-eyed girl was crying her eyes out. Her cousin Ben had let the collies into the house so that he and Stormy could play with them, but her Uncle Nick had come along and spoiled all the fun by putting Jake and Leo back outside.

"Stormy," Kathleen said, as she drew her daughter onto her lap and tried to console her, "the dogs are too big to be in the house with all these people. Besides, you don't want them to eat your pretty birthday cake!"

The child pointed her arm in the direction of the door and sobbed.

"She knows what she wants, Kathleen," Ella said as she moved through the room with a tray of snacks and drinks. "Maybe if you took her outside and let her see the dogs for a minute or two, she'd be satisfied."

"Mom, that would be spoiling her," Sam put in.

Ella looked smugly over at her son who had Olivia, now six months pregnant, cuddled in the crook of his arm.

"Oh, and I'm sure once yours gets here, you're not going to spoil it at all," she said dryly.

Sam patted Olivia's rounded tummy. "Not at all," he assured his mother, then looked across the room at his brother, who was presently dancing with a pregnant Allison. "You're not either, are you, Nick?"

Laughing, Nick kissed his wife's cheek. "What? Spoil our coming baby? Not at all! We don't spoil Ben, and we won't spoil this one. We'll raise them all with army discipline. Right, Allison?"

This brought a howl of laughter from everyone in the room.

"Right, Nick, that's why Ben sneaked around to the front parlor and let the dogs in," Allison told him.

Ross reached over and took Stormy from Kathleen's lap, which had become nearly nonexistent these past few weeks. Much to everyone's joy and wonder, Kathleen had not only conceived, she was eight-and-a-half-months pregnant and expected to deliver any day now. Proving to the doctors, and her family, that love was what really made babies.

"Well, Kathleen and I can't say we won't spoil ours," Ross told the group. "Because Stormy is already spoiled rotten."

"She's not spoiled," S.T. contradicted proudly. "She's just a stubborn-minded Gallagher."

"Amen," Ella echoed enthusiastically as she passed glasses of milk to her expecting daughter and daughters-in-law.

Ben suddenly raced into the room and didn't stop until he reached the couch where Stormy sat crying on her daddy's lap.

"Here, Stormy." He pushed a ragged replica of a basset hound at the girl. "You can have Buddy. He's a good dog."

Stormy's tears dried instantly as she gathered the cuddly old toy in her arms and wiggled down to the floor to play.

Her eyes misty, Kathleen looked over at Ross and smiled.

"One stops crying and the other one starts," he said with wry tenderness. "What's a man to do?"

"Pray the next one will be a boy," S.T. joked.

A week later the prayer was answered.

*   *   *   *   *

HE'S MORE THAN A MAN, HE'S ONE OF OUR

UNCLE DADDY

Kasey Michaels

Gabe Logan was doing just fine raising his orphaned niece alone. He didn't need or *want* any help from the baby's aunt, Erica Fletcher. Gabe could see that the uptight businesswoman didn't have a clue about child rearing. So when Erica suggested Gabe teach her about parenting, it was an offer he couldn't resist. Having her move into his house would surely force Erica to admit defeat. But when she set out to conquer his heart...Gabe knew he was in big trouble!

Find out the true meaning of *close quarters* in Kasey Michaels's UNCLE DADDY, available in February.

Fall in love with our **Fabulous Fathers**—and join the Silhouette Romance family!

FF293

**Three All-American beauties discover
love comes in all shapes and sizes!**

ALL-AMERICAN SWEETHEARTS

by Laurie Paige

CARA'S BELOVED (#917)—*February*

SALLY'S BEAU (#923)—*March*

VICTORIA'S CONQUEST (#933)—*April*

A lost love, a new love and a hidden one, three
All-American Sweethearts get their men in Paradise Falls,
West Virginia. Only in America...and only
from Silhouette Romance!

Silhouette
R O M A N C E™

Take 4 bestselling love stories FREE
Plus get a FREE surprise gift!

SMYTHESHIRE, MASSACHUSETTS.

Small town. Big secrets.

Silhouette Romance invites you to visit Elizabeth August's
small town, a place with a legacy rooted deep
in the past....

THE VIRGIN WIFE
February 1993
Madaline MacGreggor-Smythe lived a far-from-ordinary exis-
tence. Though married, she had never experienced romantic in-
timacy and probably never would. But when Colin Darnell—a man
from Madaline's past—returns to town, feelings long denied are
rekindled. And so is the danger that had separated them!

HAUNTED HUSBAND
March 1993—FABULOUS FATHERS
Thatcher Brant, widower and father of two, vowed never to love
again. This chief of police would not risk his feelings, or those of
his children, for anyone. Least of all, Samantha Hogan. But
something had told Samantha that Thatcher was the husband
for her!

SMYTHESHIRE, MASSACHUSETTS—this sleepy little town has
plenty to keep you up at night. Only from Silhouette Romance!

Silhouette
R O M A N C E™